WEB OF DECEIT

Dewey Webb Historical Mysteries, Book 1

RENÉE PAWLISH

Web of Deceit
A Dewey Webb Mystery

Published by Creative Cat Press
copyright 2016 by Renée Pawlish

ACKNOWLEDGMENTS

The author gratefully acknowledges all those who helped in the writing of this book, especially: Beth Treat, for superior editing; L & L Coins & Stamps Incorporated for coin collecting advice (any mistakes are mine, not theirs); Janice Horne, for countless hours helping me work through story ideas; and Gerry Nelson, a wonderful storyteller in his own right, for giving me insights into Denver in the 1940s. If I've forgotten anyone, please accept my apologies.

To all my beta readers: I am in your debt!

Dan Armstrong, Bill Baker, Pam Balog, Suzanne S. Barnhill, Elva Bartlett, Van Brollini, Wanda Bryant, Gia Cantwell, Jan Carrico, Irene David, Kate Dionne, Fredette DuPont, Lisa Gall, Chance Gardner, Tracy Gestewitz, Patti Gross, Barbara Hackel, Theresa Hale, Gloria Healey, Meredith Hillenbrand, Valorie Hunter, Dan Ianni, Wallace Inman, Joyce Kahaly, Kay, David King, Ray Kline, Maxine Lauer, Patrick Lyons, Linda Marchant, Lyric McKnight, Debbie McNally, Karen Melde, Becky

Neilsen, Ronnie Nelson, Janice Paysinger, Iain Picton, Yvonne Plyler, Charleen Pruett, Dave Richard, Tracie Ann Setliff, Marie Severns, Lynn Short, Bev Smith, Janet Soper, Latonya Stewart, Joyce Stumpff, Morris Sweet, Jennifer Thompson, Patricia Thursby, Barry Weisbord, Sharon Williams, Lu Wilmot

CHAPTER ONE

I'd never heard of Gordon Sandalwood until he walked up to my booth at State Bar & Grill and slid into the seat across from me.

"This table's taken, bub," I said. I had been enjoying my lunch while I read *The Denver Post* – four years after the war and there was still trouble in Germany – and I wasn't in the mood to be disturbed. Reminders of the war tended to leave me with a foul disposition.

"Dewey Webb?" he asked, but it wasn't a question. He knew who I was.

I leaned back and contemplated him. He was neat and tidy, in a gray suit and a white shirt with blue stripes, a blue tie and a gray wool trilby hat. A gray tweed overcoat was draped over one arm. I'm sure people instinctively called him 'Sir.' "

"Okay, you know my name," I finally said. *I* wasn't going to say 'Sir.' I hadn't done that since I was in the army. "How about telling me yours?"

"Gordon Sandalwood."

He took off his hat and set it and the overcoat on the seat

next to him, then reached a thin hand across the table. I waited just long enough so he'd know I was still annoyed that he was interrupting me, then firmly shook the hand.

"Okay." I pointed a finger at him. "Now I know who you are. What do you want?"

"I need a moment of your time, Mr. Webb," he said.

I gestured at my hot roast beef sandwich. "Can't it wait?"

He sighed heavily. "You're a private investigator, and I need your help."

"Why not come to my office?" After the war, I'd been an investigator for a law firm, but a year ago, I'd gone out on my own. I had a place on Sherman Street in an old Victorian house that had been converted to offices. It wasn't much, but it was private, and it was where I *should* be conducting business.

He shook his head as he took out a Chesterfield and lit it. He blew smoke off to the side, then said, "I did. Twice. I got as far as your door, but couldn't bring myself to go in. The second time, I ran into you in the hallway, but I didn't say anything."

I gave him a good once-over. "I remember you. It was last week, right?" He'd been dressed in brown that time, from his shoes to his hat. I wondered if he was always perfectly color-coordinated.

He nodded. "Then today, I'd finally screwed up my courage to talk to you, but when I got to your office, you were just leaving. So I followed you here."

I folded up my paper and pushed it aside. The article about Ted Williams winning the AL MVP would have to wait. "It must be something important if it couldn't wait any longer."

"It is." His face twisted up with a pained expression. "It's not easy to ask for help."

"But you're here, so shoot."

"It's my wife."

2

I folded my arms, beginning to lose patience with him. "I'm listening."

He tamped out the barely smoked cigarette in a tin ashtray, then pulled out a leather wallet. He extracted a picture and handed it to me. "Her name is Edith. She's twenty-nine, two years younger than me."

I studied the black-and-white photo. Edith was a good-looking dame, with a round face, light hair, big dark eyes, and full lips spread into a light smile.

"She's pretty," I said noncommittally as I handed the picture back to him.

He put the picture back in his wallet. "That was taken a few years ago. She was a lot happier then."

"What happened?"

He shrugged, then rested his hands on the table and tapped his fingertips together. "I wish I knew. Lately she's not been herself. She doesn't smile or laugh anymore. When I ask her if she's okay, she tells me she's fine, but I know she's not."

"Have you considered taking her to a psychoanalyst?"

"I mentioned that once and she got mad at me and repeated that she was okay. And for a day or two, she seemed better. But then she started acting strange again."

"How so?"

"I work at the Federal Center. I'm an engineer, with regular hours. I leave work at five and come home the same time every night. She always has dinner on the table when I get home. She's a good cook." His face momentarily lit up with pride. "But for the past two weeks, she's been rushing around in the kitchen when I get home, trying to get dinner ready. That's not like her. When I ask her why the rush, she says she got busy out in the yard, or talking to our neighbor Jane, and she lost track of the time."

3

"It's December," I said, "and it snowed a week ago. What kind of yard work is she doing?"

He held up a hand. "I don't know. I couldn't tell that anything had been done in the yard. And I ran into Jane one morning and joked about how she was keeping Edith from her chores. Jane looked at me like I was crazy and said she hadn't talked to Edith in a week, that Edith's been gone a lot during the day."

"Was Jane lying to you?"

"I don't think so, and why would she?"

"Just asking the question."

He took out another cigarette, but instead of lighting it, he fiddled with it. "After Jane told me that, I talked to another neighbor, Irene. She has two boys, and that keeps her busy. She also said she hasn't talked to Edith in a while, which is unusual."

"Has she *seen* Edith? Working in the yard, maybe?"

"Irene didn't say, but if she did, they probably would've talked."

"Do you believe Irene?"

"I think so. I don't know why she'd lie to me." He kept playing with the cigarette.

"How well do you know the neighbors?"

He shrugged. "It's been four years. We moved here after the war, when I got hired at the Federal Center. During the war, Edith lived with her sister in Limon. Edith's sister was a schoolteacher there, but she moved here three years ago."

"So you've lived here long enough that Edith should know your neighbors fairly well."

"I would think so."

"Did Edith work while you were overseas?"

"She worked for a while at a small grocery store in Limon, and she helped her sister. But she hasn't worked since I came home and we moved here."

4

"What does Edith do when you're at work?"

"She grocery shops on Mondays. Wednesdays she has bridge club. She has other errands, and keeps up with the housework, and cooks."

"You don't have kids?"

The pain flashed on his face again. "No. Edith...can't have children."

That could make any woman sad, I thought. My wife, Clara, hadn't conceived right away, and I had seen how that had worn on her. Our son, Sam, was three months old and I knew how much being a mother meant to Clara. "Uh-huh," I murmured.

He continued, as if that sensitive topic had never been brought up. "And the past two days, I've called her from work, but she doesn't answer."

"She wasn't shopping or at bridge?"

He shook his head. "I called when she should've been around, but she wasn't. Both nights, when I got home, I asked her about it. She lied and said she must've been out in the yard and didn't hear the phone. But I tried calling for hours."

"And no answer."

"Right."

I studied him. "And you have no idea where she might've been?"

"None."

I leaned forward, then cleared my throat. "I don't want to seem forward, but do you think your wife's having an affair?"

"No. We love each other." His voice was tight.

Because of the question, or because he thought the affair was possible? I wondered.

"I had to ask," I said. He didn't say anything to that. "How long have you been married?"

"Almost eight years. We met a few months before Pearl Harbor. After the Japs attacked us, I enlisted. We got married right before I left." He gazed out the window. "It was hard on her, while I was gone. She was...lonely, I think, even though her sister was around."

"Times were tough," I said. I hadn't met Clara until after the war, but I knew of a lot of men who married their sweethearts and then immediately left for the war. And many never returned.

He turned back to me. "When I came home after the war, things got better. We've been happy. Until lately."

"And you can't think of any other reason your wife's acting like this?"

He shook his head.

"Does she have any money?"

"She has a weekly budget for groceries, gas, that sort of thing."

"And nothing's missing from your bank account?"

"No, nothing like that."

I took a long moment to think about it. "It's not a lot to go on," I said.

He sighed. "I realize that. That's why I want to hire you. Find out what Edith's doing. Follow her and see where she goes. I can't do it because I have to work, and besides, she might see me and then she'd be even more careful about whatever she's doing." He slipped some twenties across the table. "That should get you started."

I sipped my Coke, then picked up the bills and stuffed them in my pocket. "Okay. I'll watch your wife tomorrow and see what happens. Then we'll talk."

He nodded. "Maybe you'll find out something."

"Where can I reach you?"

He pulled a card from his wallet. It had his name, office address, and phone number on it. "You can reach me at work."

"Where do you live?"

"You can't talk to me there or Edith might get suspicious," he said quickly.

I cocked an eyebrow at him. "If I'm going to follow her, I need to know where you live."

He choked out a laugh. "Oh, yes, of course." He gave me an address on King Street near Sloans Lake, west of downtown. Most of the houses in the area were 1920s-style bungalows with detached garages. "I leave for work at seven-thirty, and she never leaves before I do."

"Does she have a car?"

"Yes, we have a Chrysler. I take the streetcar to work."

"I'll be there tomorrow morning," I said. "And we'll see what happens."

"Excellent." With that, he slid out of the booth. "I'll expect a call from you late tomorrow," he said as he donned his hat and overcoat. Then he strode out of the restaurant.

I grabbed my sandwich, cold by now, and finished it, then put two quarters on the table and left for my office. I needed to start a file on Gordon Sandalwood, and then finish some paperwork and pay some bills. The money Sandalwood had given me would help with that, although I didn't see it going too far. This case wouldn't take too long. It'd be simple, I thought, probably a misunderstanding between them, or maybe I'd discover that Edith was having an affair.

I'd look back on this moment and realize how wrong I'd been.

CHAPTER TWO

At seven o'clock the next morning, I was parked in my black Plymouth sedan down the street from the Sandalwood home. It was a red-brick bungalow with yellow trim, a long driveway that led to a detached garage at the back of the house, a sidewalk that cut through a small yard, and concrete steps up to a porch that spanned the length of the house. Two rocking chairs sat to the right of the front door. I wondered how often Gordon and Edith sat there.

I sank down low in my seat, pulled my hat forward to shield my face, and waited. A few minutes later, a green Mercury coupe drove past me, but the driver — a man in a tan Homburg — didn't even notice me. Five minutes after that, two small boys came out of a house next door to the Sandalwoods, books under their arms, lunch pails swinging from small hands. A woman in a tan dress came onto the porch and waved at them, then disappeared back in the house. I watched the boys in my rearview mirror as they ambled toward Seventeenth, and I pictured my son Sam someday walking to school like them. Then the street grew quiet and no one paid me any mind. I'd shut off the engine so I wouldn't draw attention to myself, but now a chill crept into the car. I crossed my arms to keep warm.

At seven-thirty, Sandalwood emerged from his house. He was smartly dressed in a brown suit and matching brown fedora, and today he wore a brown overcoat. I hoped he wouldn't see me, so that he wouldn't subconsciously do something that would alert Edith to my presence. But Sandalwood walked down the steps toward the street and didn't look my way. Instead, he adjusted his hat, then turned right and hurried in the opposite direction, toward Colfax. A moment later, I lost sight of him.

I lit a cigarette and slowly smoked it. Boredom set in. I looked around and caught my reflection in the side mirror, then glanced away. I'm okay looking, with light hair I'd grown out a bit from my military buzz cut, and a square face, but I don't like seeing myself, especially my eyes. Clara says my eyes are older than my twenty-nine years. That's what came from seeing what I'd seen during the war. Nobody talked about their war experiences in any detail, but we all knew and recognized the haunting that came from them. The war was still near to me, nearer than I liked. I never told anybody, but I hoped the images that still flashed in my mind would someday fade.

Somewhere a dog barked and brought me back to the present. As the sun rose, it warmed the inside of the Plymouth a little bit and I found myself growing drowsy. The morning dragged on. I remembered too many days like this during the war. The waiting and wondering was almost as bad as the combat itself, because you knew what was coming, and it wasn't going to be good.

Finally at eleven, a blue Chrysler Windsor slowly backed down the Sandalwood driveway. A woman with flaxen hair in a pageboy style was inside. Edith, I presumed. I ducked down, then glanced over the dashboard. The Chrysler reached the street, then headed south. When it reached the corner of West Sixteenth and King, I popped my head back up, started the Plymouth and eased into the street. I got to Sixteenth and saw the Chrysler turning east onto Colfax. I stayed back, but it was easy to follow Edith, as she didn't drive very fast. I let three cars get between her and me as we drove east. We soon passed downtown and continued on Colfax until we reached Josephine Street. She turned north, then right on Seventeenth. On our left side was City Park, 330 acres of grass and trees, with two lakes, the City Park Pavilion, and a boathouse. She then took a left into the park. I waited for a car to pass by on Seventeenth, then followed her. The road split into a Y, and the Chrysler veered left. I crept up to the intersection, then checked my rearview mirror. No one was behind me, so I edged forward. Through some trees I could see Ferril Lake, the bigger of the park's two lakes. I looked to the left, down the road. The Chrysler was a hundred feet ahead of me. I waited a moment, then turned the wheel and drove slowly after it. The day was chilly, and few people were in the park.

Edith soon parked near the Pavilion, a large, yellow-brick Spanish-style building with twin towers, arches, and a red roof. I pulled up to the side of the road behind a Woody station wagon and watched the Chrysler. The driver's door opened and Edith got out. She wore a blue dress that accentuated her curvy figure, black heels, and a blue pillbox hat. She pulled on a white trench coat, adjusted her stockings, and then strode across the road. She glanced around and I sank down low, but since I'd parked behind another car, I doubted she would see me.

I'd brought my Bausch & Lomb binoculars with me, and I pulled them out of the leather case and focused on Edith. She walked down a path between a grove of maple trees, her hair shimmering in the light, then emerged into an open space. She stopped at a bench, then glanced all around again, and finally sat down hesitantly. She placed her purse next to her and put her hands in her lap. Low hazy clouds obliterated the sun, and she cinched the belt of her coat tightly around her waist. Her full lips had formed a hard line and she began fidgeting with the hem of her coat. Then she suddenly stood up and stared to her left. I swung the binoculars in that direction.

A man in a dark coat and black pork pie hat appeared through the trees. He had brown hair, a thin mustache, and a long beak for a nose. He narrowed his eyes, then started toward Edith. As he neared her, Edith said something and they both sat down on the bench. They began talking, and Edith was gesturing at him. He nodded and held up his hands, then said something else. Edith put a hand on his arm, and he pulled away from her. Whatever he said next made Edith's face pinch up. Her lower lip quivered as she responded. He shook his head and started to rise. Edith grabbed his coat and pulled him back down. Then she grabbed her purse, opened it, and yanked out an envelope. She handed it to the man. He opened it and checked its contents, then shoved it into his coat pocket and stood up. He said something else, and Edith grabbed his arm again. He shrugged her off, spun around, and stalked back toward the trees. Edith leaped to her feet and called after him. Her purse fell to the ground, spilling its contents. But the man ignored her, and he soon disappeared. Edith stood for a moment, her eyes wide. Then she bent down, and as she scooped up the contents of her purse, she wept. She threw everything back in the purse and sat back down on the bench. She took some deep breaths, dabbed at her eyes with a handkerchief, fixed her makeup, then stood up and hurried back through the trees to the Chrysler. She got in and the car soon pulled onto the road. I waited a moment before following her. The road was deserted, so I stayed back where I could just see her car.

Edith headed into a roundabout, then drove south. At Colfax, she turned west. I fell in behind her, again keeping cars between us. A half-hour later, she was back home. I parked in a different place from the morning, and resumed watching the house. An hour passed while I listened to a jazz station, but nothing happened. I smoked a few cigarettes and tapped the steering wheel. Then I ate a peanut butter and jelly sandwich that Clara had fixed for me this morning. The next-door neighbor that I'd seen this morning walked over and knocked on the Sandalwood door. A moment later, Edith opened it. She smiled warmly and stepped aside to let the neighbor in. I took that opportunity to drive around the block. When I returned, I parked on the corner where I could still see the Sandalwood house. The afternoon dragged on. I checked my watch. Three o'clock. Then the Sandalwood front door opened and the neighbor left, just in time for children who were arriving home from school. I waited until four, then smoked the last of too many cigarettes on this stakeout. I doubted Edith would leave the house now, since her husband would be coming home soon. I was tired and bored, and I'd seen as much as I was going to today, so I fired up the Plymouth and left.

CHAPTER THREE

I headed down King Street to Colfax, then drove west until I found a Conoco station. I pulled in, parked, and trotted inside.

A guy behind a counter near the entrance threw me a bored look. I bought a pack of cigarettes, then strolled back outside. Near the entrance was a pay phone. I took out the card Sandalwood had given me. Then I picked up the receiver, shoved a nickel into the phone, and dialed his number.

"This is Sandalwood," he answered.

"It's Dewey Webb," I said.

"I've been waiting for your call." He lowered his voice. "Did you see anything? What'd she do today?" He was part eager, part desperate.

"She went out." I told him about his wife meeting the mysterious stranger in the park.

"Who was the guy?" he asked.

"Beats me." I described the man in detail. "Do you know him?"

"He doesn't sound like anyone I know, or Edith, for that matter."

I paused as a delivery truck rattled down Colfax, then said, "You're sure Edith's not having an affair?" It was blunt, but I was stiff from sitting so long, and I didn't feel like being tactful.

"Well..." He didn't say anything for a long moment. "No, I don't buy it. She's been faithful to me."

I drummed my fingers on top of the pay phone, wondering if that was wishful thinking on his part.

"What was in the envelope she gave the guy?" he asked.

"I was too far away to see anything, but my guess would be money."

"Why would she be paying him?"

"To not reveal an affair to you?"

"No, that's not it," he insisted. He groaned into the phone. "This doesn't make any sense."

"Is there anything you're not telling me? Is your wife in some kind of trouble? She was certainly upset when she talked to that man."

"No," he said vehemently. "I don't know what's going on."

He seemed sincere, but I was naturally distrustful, and I didn't know whether to believe him or not.

"Is there anyone I can talk to about her?" I asked.

"If you do, she'll get suspicious and she'll be more careful. Then I'll never find out what's going on. You'll have to follow her again."

I sucked a breath in. I didn't relish the idea of another stakeout. "I can't watch your house day after day. Someone will get suspicious."

"Tomorrow's Saturday," he said. "We'll be home for the weekend, so come back Monday. And I want you to find the man she met."

I frowned. "How am I going to do that? I have no idea who he is."

16

"Maybe Edith will meet him again. I'll pay you for your time."

I ran a hand over my jaw. I didn't see this going anywhere, but I was also at loose ends at the moment. "Okay, it's your money."

"Good."

"Is there anything else you can tell me about Edith?" I asked. "Anything out of the ordinary."

"Not really. She stays busy during the day, and at night we listen to the radio or read. She's close to her sister and..." He stopped.

"What?"

"Come to think of it, Edith has been talking to Ruby a lot more lately."

"Ruby? That's Edith's sister?"

"Yes. They're pretty close, and they usually talk about once a week. But lately it's been almost every night."

"Maybe Ruby knows something," I said. "Did you ask her?"

"I asked her at Thanksgiving if something was going on with Edith. She laughed it off and said it must be my imagination. If I ask again, she'll say something to Edith."

"Would that be a bad thing?"

"I told you, Edith would be that much more careful about whatever's going on, and I won't find out what has her so upset."

"You're tying my hands," I said.

"What do you mean?"

"You don't want to talk to anybody about Edith, and you don't want *me* to talk to anybody about her. It makes it hard to find out what's going on."

"I'm sure you're up to the task."

I swallowed a retort. "I'll be there Monday morning. If nothing happens, I'm out."

17

"Fine, thank you."

I hung up the phone and walked slowly back to my car. I kept thinking about Edith. What did she give that man, and why was she so distraught afterward?

————

Monday morning, I was again parked down the street from the Sandalwood house. I didn't want to spend the day on another stakeout, and my mood reflected that. I'd snapped at Clara that morning before I left home, and it didn't help that it was a cloudy, blustery day. I wasn't looking forward to freezing in my car.

Promptly at seven-thirty, Sandalwood emerged from his house. As I would've expected, he was neatly dressed, this time in black. He jammed his hat onto his head, then walked down the steps and glanced up and down the street. But instead of heading toward Colfax, he spotted me in the Plymouth and locked eyes with me. He subtly nodded at me, then carefully signaled to the south. He started down the block, and a few houses down, he glanced over his shoulder and nodded his head again.

I cranked the engine and drove the Plymouth past him. He quickly pointed ahead. I reached the corner and crossed the intersection, then parked halfway down the next block. A minute later, he approached the car. I leaned across the seat and rolled down the passenger window.

"Are you nuts?" I snapped as he bent down and put his face into the window. "What if she saw you?" I glanced back toward his house. No one was outside.

"Relax. She was in the bathtub when I left." His overcoat whipped around as he talked.

"You hope."

He held up a hand to silence me. "I needed to talk to you."

I looked back toward his house again. Still no Edith. "Make it quick."

"When I got home Friday night, Edith was clearly upset. She tried to hide it, but she was on edge all weekend. Something is definitely not right. "

"We know that."

He shook his head. "This was even more so. Whatever happened with that man has her really upset. And last night, after I went to bed, Edith got up and I overheard her talking to her sister on the phone. Edith said something about being in real trouble, and she needed the Gaudens that Ruby has."

"What's the Gaudens?"

He shrugged. "I have no idea. Edith is meeting Ruby at the Rexall at 3:30 today, so maybe you can find out what it is."

"Which Rexall?"

"Edith didn't say, but Ruby teaches near Pierce and Twenty-fourth. There's a Rexall near there, on Twentieth, so that's probably the one."

I nodded. "Fine." Then I gestured at him. "Now get going, before Edith sees you talking to me."

He reached into the car and handed me a piece of paper. "That's my home phone. If you can't call me at the office, call the house. I want to know what happens."

"I will." I folded the paper and put it in my coat pocket.

"I'll miss my ride," he said. He gave me a quick wave, ran down the street, and disappeared.

CHAPTER FOUR

I waited until Sandalwood disappeared on Colfax, then I drove around the block and parked in a different spot than before. I was a little worried that someone might get wise to the Plymouth being on the street again, but it was a chance I'd have to take. I took off my hat and sank down low in the seat so I wouldn't be easily spotted, and then I waited. And waited. I ate a sandwich, and waited some more.

Nothing happened until 3:30, when the Sandalwood Chrysler backed out of the driveway and headed down the street to Colfax. I followed as Edith drove straight to Pierce, then north to Twentieth Street, less than ten minutes away. On the corner was a white building with an orange-and-blue Rexall Drugs sign. Rexall sponsored a lot of radio shows, like *Amos 'n' Andy* and the *Jimmy Durante Show*, and every time I saw a Rexall Drugstore, their radio greeting rang in my head: "Good health to all from Rexall."

Edith parked in the lot in front of the Rexall and got out. She was easy to spot in her stylish white trench coat. I drove past the store, pulled a U-turn, and zipped into the lot. Edith was just entering the building. I pulled into a space a few down from her Chrysler and trotted after her.

I stepped through the door and glanced around. To the left were aisles and shelves full of cosmetics, gifts, and magazines. At the back was the pharmacy, and along the wall to the right was a long lunch counter with pink barstools. A baldheaded man bustled around behind the counter, fixing floats for a group of high school students who were gathered at the far end of the counter. Edith was perched on a barstool closer to the entrance, staring into a mirror on the wall behind the counter. She'd taken off her coat and placed it and her purse on the stool next to her.

An old man with a wheezing cough jostled past me and strode back to the pharmacy, and a woman with bags in both hands headed for the entrance. I held the door open for her, then moved over to the lunch counter and slid onto a stool three away from Edith. I pushed my hat back on my head and looked at her out of the corner of my eye. She'd never seen me before, and she gave me no notice. The baldheaded man finished fixing floats for the high-schoolers and he moseyed down to our end.

"What can I get you?" he asked Edith. She was oblivious to him. "Ma'am?" he said to her.

She jumped and looked at him. "Oh...a cup of coffee, please." She had a silky voice that reminded me of Ava Gardner, but right now it had an uneasy tinge to it.

His eyes fell on me.

"Coffee," I said.

He nodded, then quickly poured cups of coffee for her and me. He clinked them down on the counter and walked away. I sipped my coffee and studied Edith in the mirror behind the counter. She wore a gray dress with lace today, with a flowered hat and gloves. Any other time I'd have said she was a dreamboat, but her frown and the sadness in her eyes tarnished an otherwise perfect face and outfit. She stared into the mirror without seeming to see anything.

An old newspaper lay on the counter nearby, so I set my cup down and grabbed it. I pretended to read it while I watched her in the mirror. She didn't touch her coffee. A minute later, the door opened and a woman flew in along with a blast of cold air. She looked around, then strode purposefully over to Edith. She pecked Edith on the cheek and sat on the stool on the other side of her.

Ruby, I presumed. She was a full-figured dish, about ten years older than Edith, with shoulder-length blond hair that included a generous amount of gray, smooth skin, and the same full lips as her sister. But the dark eyes that stared at her sister were cold and hard.

"Sorry I'm late." Ruby's voice was low and rushed. "I couldn't get away."

The guy behind the counter started to approach them, but Ruby warned him away with a wave of her hand and an icy glare. People came and went, but they didn't notice any of it.

"It's all right," Edith murmured.

"So," Ruby said breathlessly. "Did you hear anything today?"

Edith shook her head. "No, but why would I?" She paused. "I'm worried."

"I can't believe you went alone." Ruby put a hand to her lips in a pensive way, as if she was paying close attention to every word being said.

"I didn't have a choice."

Ruby took in a breath and let it out slowly, as if to calm herself. "This man, who was he?"

"I don't know. I've never seen him before."

"Did he tell you his name?"

"No."

"Let me see the note."

Edith pulled a piece of paper from her purse and slid it across to Ruby. Ruby picked it up, read it, and frowned. Then she handed the note back to Edith.

"Why didn't you tell me about this before?" Ruby asked.

"I...hoped it was some kind of joke, that it would go away."

"Clearly it wasn't and it hasn't."

"Please, Ruby, I need your help."

Ruby wagged her head wearily. "Does it ever change?"

"Please," Edith whispered. "Don't chastise me, not now."

Ruby frowned, her hand at her mouth, and her eyes softened. She reached out and squeezed Edith's hand. "It'll be all right."

"I don't know." Edith choked up. "Gordon can't find out what happened. It'll ruin us, and I don't want that."

They lapsed into silence.

"Would the Pattersons have told anyone?" Edith finally asked.

"No," Ruby said emphatically.

"You're sure?"

"We can trust them."

"*Someone* knows."

Ruby let out a heavy sigh. "I just don't understand. We were outside of town, and we were careful."

The women sat in silence again, this time for a full minute. They were oblivious to the hustle and bustle around them. Then it was Ruby's turn to pull something from her purse. It was small and flat, but I couldn't see what it was.

"Here," she said.

Edith took it. "Thank you."

"Be careful with it," Ruby said.

"I will." Edith gingerly put the object in her purse. It looked like it was made of plastic. "I'll take it to the shop now."

Ruby nodded. "I hope it's worth it."

"It is." Edith sighed. "It breaks my heart to have to do this now. He never got rid of these before, even though he had offers..." Her voice trailed off.

Ruby touched Edith's arm. "This has to be it, Edith. We can't let go of any more of them. You let this man know that."

"I know." Edith's lower lip quivered. "I'll make it up to you, somehow."

"It's okay. I didn't abandon you before, and I won't now."

"You were a trouper."

Ruby sighed. "That's me, the trouper." The frown appeared again, and she again raked her hands through her hair. "When do you have to give him the money?"

"The day after tomorrow, at noon."

"I'll go with you."

Edith shook her head. "I have to meet him again at City Park. You'll be at school."

"I don't like the idea of you going out there alone."

"I'll be fine, Ruby. He's not going to do anything to me, because he wants the money."

"I'm worried about what he'll do *after* you give him the money."

"I'll be fine," Edith said, but her voice trembled.

"I want you to come by the school afterward so I know you're okay."

"I will."

"I know about bad men," Ruby continued to chide her. "You think you're out of their clutches, and they come back."

"Oh no, has Lester been around?" Edith asked.

Ruby let out a bitter laugh. "No, and if I'm lucky, it'll stay that way." She glanced sideways at Edith. "For the life of me, you have someone as good as Gordon, and –"

"Don't start, Ruby."

"I'm sorry," Ruby said.

Edith slipped off the stool and shrugged into her coat. "I'd better hurry before the store closes." She grabbed her purse, took out some change, and plopped it on the counter. "And I need to get back home before Gordon does."

I quickly paid for my coffee and sauntered for the door.

"Call me," Ruby said to Edith as I passed by them.

When I got outside, I ran through a chilly breeze to the Plymouth, hopped in, and then watched the store entrance. The two women had just emerged. Ruby walked in the other direction to an old gray Chevy, while Edith headed for the Chrysler. She got in and a moment later drove out of the parking lot with me behind her. I let cars get between us and tailed her east on Colfax to Broadway. She turned south and a mile down the road, she pulled to the curb in front of a warehouse on the right. I went past her and parked in a space near the corner. Edith hopped out of the car and dashed across the street, one hand clutching her purse, the other holding her hat in place. She paused in front of a store with wide windows. A sign painted on one of the windows read "Denver Stamp and Coin." She hesitated, then went inside.

Cars passed back and forth along Broadway. I checked my watch. 4:20. I wanted to go inside to see what Edith was doing, but since I'd just sat down next to her at the Rexall, I couldn't risk it. Even though she hadn't appeared to be paying attention, she still might recognize me. I lit a cigarette, but I hadn't smoked much of it before Edith walked back out of Denver Stamp and Coin. She looked left and right, then dodged cars as she ran back to the Chrysler. A moment later, she passed by me, but this time I didn't follow. Edith would be heading home so she could arrive before Gordon. I doubted I'd find anything revealing by going after her. I might, however, find information inside Denver Stamp and Coin.

CHAPTER FIVE

Wind whipped at me as I ran across the street to Denver Stamp and Coin, but when I raced into the store, warmth enveloped me. A man in a tweed overcoat was just stepping toward the door.

"Thanks, Cecil," he called out. "I'll be back soon."

Somewhere in the back, a voice murmured a goodbye. I held the door open and the man stepped out into the cold. I glanced around. Wood-and-glass display cases ran in rows throughout the store, some filled with stamps, others with coins in small plastic cases and coin boards. Wartime advertising posters, with sayings such as "For Victory Buy United States War Savings Bonds Stamps" hung on one wall, but the other wood-paneled walls were bare. The store was packed full, but it was tidy.

I sidled between display cases to the back, where a man with light gray hair sat at a desk behind another row of display cases. An old Philco radio on his desk played big-band music. The man looked up over wire-rimmed glasses and saw me.

"Oh, hello." He reached over with a long arm and turned a knob on the radio, and the music faded. "How can I help you?"

I took off my hat and nodded. "I need a little information."

He slid out of his chair and moved around the desk. He was tall, a little over my six feet, and wiry. I leaned against the display case casually.

"You have a question about a coin or stamp?" His voice was smooth and cultured, with the hint of a British accent.

I shook my head. "A dame."

His eyebrows rose in surprise and he pushed his glasses farther up his large nose. "A dame stamp? Or do you mean a coin?" He gestured at the display cases. "We have a wide selection, but I don't think I've ever heard of such a thing."

I shook my head. "No, a dame was in here, a few minutes ago. A blonde. She was wearing a white overcoat." I described Edith Sandalwood. "You know who I mean?"

"Oh yes, of course." He emitted a polite little laugh. "I thought you meant a stamp. I've never heard of a stamp called the 'Dame.' I've heard of a Penny Black. That's a British penny stamp that has Queen Victoria on it, and it was printed in black."

I forced an interested smile, working him to my side. "This woman who came in, was she just looking around or..." I let my voice trail off.

He grew wary. "Why do you want to know about her?"

I pulled out my PI license and showed it to him. "I need to ask you a few questions."

"Oh, dear, is she in some kind of trouble?"

"Possibly."

He used thin fingers to push his glasses up on his forehead. "And such a nice woman."

"What did she want?"

"She sold me a coin." His jaw suddenly dropped. "It wasn't stolen, was it?"

"Not that I'm aware of," I said, although I really didn't know where Ruby had gotten it. "What coin did she have?"

"A twenty-dollar gold piece." He turned around and picked up a small plastic case from his desk, then set it on the display case. Inside it was a shiny gold coin. "It's a St. Gaudens double eagle. It's a rare piece. It was designed by the sculptor Augustus Saint Gaudens. Theodore Roosevelt commissioned him to design the coin because Roosevelt thought what we had was boring."

"Right." I cut him off before he went on about the history of the coin. "How much is it worth?"

"Close to a thousand dollars. She wanted top dollar because she said she had to pay off a loan, but I paid her a bit less than that because I have to make a profit." He resumed his lecture. "These double eagles are rare, in part because the government melted a lot of them in the late '30s. Now, if one had a St. Gaudens that was minted in 1933, those are *really* rare."

I interrupted him again. "Has she been in here before? Selling other coins?"

He shook his head. "No, I've never seen her, although she said her father used to come in."

"Her father?"

"Yes. John Norland. He was a collector."

"Was?"

"Yes. He passed before the war. Heart attack. And such a nice man. He was a doctor. He lived in Limon, but every time he came into Denver, he'd come by the shop and we'd talk, and he usually bought or sold something. I assume she inherited the coin from him."

"That makes sense," I said. "Did Norland have a big collection?"

"I never saw it, but I think so."

"Did Norland own a lot of St. Gaudens coins?"

"I'm not sure. It's possible he had more."

"If the coin you bought was from his collection, do you know where he might have gotten it?"

"I don't know."

"How much was his collection worth?"

"I don't know, but he'd been collecting for years, so it probably had some value." He pulled out a pocket watch and made a show of checking it. "Excuse me. I close at five."

"And Norland's daughter only came in today?"

He nodded. "That's the only time I've seen her."

"What about another woman with blond hair?" I described Ruby. "Does she sound familiar?"

He thought for a moment. "No, I don't think so. I don't have a lot of women coming in here." With that, he came around the display cases and walked me to the entrance.

I opened the door, but before I stepped out into the cold, I pulled out a card with my office number on it and handed it to him. "If that woman comes in again, would you mind calling me?"

"I guess I can do that." He pocketed the card. "Have a good evening."

"Thanks, Mac." But the door was already closing.

The skies were a steel gray and the temperature was quickly dropping. I dodged cars on Broadway as I ran back to the Plymouth. I hopped in and checked the time: a few minutes after five. Sandalwood would be on his way home, so I drove back to King Street and parked on the corner, where I could watch Colfax. Darkness settled in, and ten minutes later, a streetcar stopped across the street and down a block. A bunch of men in suits, overcoats, and hats got off. A few of them waited for a lull in traffic, then dashed across Colfax. As they passed under a streetlight, I saw Gordon Sandalwood. He strode along Colfax, his head down, and turned onto King. I rolled down the window and called to him. He jumped before he realized it was me.

"What're you doing here?" he asked.

I jerked my head toward the passenger seat. "Get in."

He hurried over and got in. "It's cold," he said as he rubbed his hands together. "What happened with Edith and Ruby? Did you go to the Rexall?"

"Yeah. I overheard them talking."

He turned so he could see me. "And?"

"Edith didn't know the man that she met," I said. "It looks like she's paying him off." I explained about the coin and Edith having to meet with the guy again.

His eyebrows furrowed into a single line. "What has she gotten herself into?"

"Whatever it is, she doesn't want you to know about it. She told Ruby that."

That small consolation didn't seem to lift his spirits. He hung his head and whispered, "I just don't understand why she won't talk to me."

"Maybe it's time to ask your wife what she's up to."

He gazed up at me. "I know her. If I do, she'll just clam up." He groaned and put his head in his hands. "When I've tried to talk to her about other...problems, she won't discuss anything, and I never know what's behind her behavior. It was like that when she couldn't get pregnant. She wouldn't talk to me about it, and it was so long before she finally told me why she was upset. If I confront her now, I don't know if she'd ever tell me why she's acting like this."

I tapped the wheel for a moment. "Are you sure you want to find out what's going on?" I finally asked. "You may not like it."

"Yes. I have to know. I'll pay you whatever it takes."

I took a deep breath. "Fine." I rubbed a hand over my chin,

then said, "Did you know that Edith and Ruby's father collected coins?"

"Edith never mentioned it."

"It sounds like he might've had quite a collection."

"That's news to me."

I thought back to the conversation I'd overheard at the drugstore. "I think Ruby has the collection now."

He shrugged. "Her father died before I met Edith and she's never talked about him much, so I don't know anything about that."

"Is her mother around?"

"No, she died when Edith was a little girl. Ruby raised her. It was just the two of them and their father."

"Have you ever heard of the Pattersons?"

He frowned. "No, should I?"

"Not necessarily. And you said that Edith stayed in Limon with her sister while you were away?"

"Yes. Why?"

"Did they live in town?"

"No, they stayed at the family house outside of town. They moved there from Kansas. Ruby sold the place when she moved to Denver, and I think she got rid of most of their father's stuff."

"Have you ever been out there?"

He shook his head. "After I came back from the war, Edith never wanted to visit, and Ruby would come to Denver to see us. I don't know anyone there, so why bother making the trip?"

"I'm going to go to Limon and ask around," I said. "It sounds like something happened out there that they don't want anyone to know about."

"It's a mystery to me." He snapped his fingers. "Maybe that fellow she met in the park is from there."

"It's possible," I said. "One more thing. Who's Lester?"

He let out a snort. "Lester Klassen. Ruby's ex-husband. They divorced three years ago. Lester drinks too much, and she's better off without him. What does he have to do with Edith?"

"Nothing," I said. "Edith asked if Ruby had heard from him, and Ruby said no."

"The only reason Lester would come back is for money, and I doubt Ruby would give him any. Like I said, he's no good."

"All right." I waved my hand back toward his house. "You better get going or Edith will wonder where you are."

"Right." He opened the door and the cold night air rushed in. "How long will you be in Limon?"

"A day or two," I said. "I'll call you when I get back."

"Good." He got out and shut the door. I waited until he disappeared into the darkness, and then I drove off.

CHAPTER SIX

Clara was in the kitchen when I got home. She poked her head into the living room and smiled at me.

"How was your day?"

"It was fine." I hung my hat on a coatrack near the door, then slipped out of my coat. We rented an old house in Barnum, a working-class neighborhood near Fourth Avenue and Federal Boulevard. The house wasn't much, a two-bedroom brick with a tiny, covered front porch and a postage-stamp-sized yard. The famous showman P. T. Barnum purchased the land in 1878, but he'd never actually lived in the neighborhood. It wasn't the best area in town, but it was what we could afford. I hoped someday I could move us to a newer development farther west.

"I've got a roast in the oven," she said as she turned back into the kitchen.

"Sounds good."

I watched her through the arched doorway. She was a few years older than me, with long, wavy brown hair clearly inspired by Veronica Lake's sultry style. Clara had been engaged during the war, but her fiancé died in the invasion at Salerno, Italy in 1943. When I met her a few years later, she was living with her parents and working as a secretary at a doctor's office. She was considered an old maid, but that hadn't mattered to me. I'd seen her eating lunch with some friends at Woolworth's. She'd looked up at me, and I saw a deep sadness in her gray eyes. I went over and said hello. We talked, and she laughed, and right away I knew that one day she'd be my wife.

Clara crossed to the stove, but she saw me staring and stopped. "What?"

I smiled. "Nothing."

She waved a hand dismissively. "Go check on Sam and make sure he's asleep, then come in to dinner."

I moseyed down a short hallway and peeked into our room, where my son Sam was asleep in a crib, a soft blanket covering him up to his neck, his delicate blond hair sticking up on his tiny head. My erratic schedule prevented me from seeing him as much as I wanted. There were too many nights when he was in bed by the time I got home. My own father – a cold, hard man – had worked long hours, a necessity born out of poverty. Midway through the Depression, when I was sixteen, he left my mother, two brothers, and me, and never came back. I vowed I would not do that to my wife and kids, but with another night of not seeing my son, I wondered if I was any better than my father. I worked too much. And I was a harder man than I wanted to be. Some of it was trained into me during the war; some of it was there already. All of it I wished I could wash away. At times, it served me well. But people sensed that coldness, and it kept them distant.

Sam stirred and I listened as he sucked on his pacifier and settled himself. I watched him for a while longer and then strolled back into the kitchen.

"I have to go to Limon tomorrow," I announced as I went to the cupboard, pulled out a glass and filled it with water, then sat down at the table.

"Oh?" Clara was moderating her tone. I could tell she was apprehensive. Even though I'd found myself in some sticky situations when I worked at the law office, she hadn't worried as much as she does now that I'm out on my own. "What's in Limon?"

"I'm not sure," I said, "just digging up some information."

"How long will you be gone?"

"I don't know. A day or two."

She fixed two plates of roast beef, potatoes, and carrots, and set them on the table. It smelled good, and after a day of peanut butter sandwiches, I was hungry. As we ate, we listened to the *Inner Sanctum Mystery* show on the radio. Clara enjoyed the scary parts and laughed at the jokes, but my mind was on Edith Sandalwood and Ruby Klassen. What were they hiding?

———

The sun was bright in my eyes as I took Highway 70 east from Denver. Limon, called the "Hub City" of eastern Colorado because multiple highways pass through the small town, is eighty miles from Denver, so I left early. I wanted to have a full day there if I needed it. The farther from Denver I drove, the more rural the landscape became, with flat farmland dotting the plains. By nine, I was driving down Main Street, past a Piggly Wiggly, the Limon Railroad Depot, and the Tompkins Hotel. I spotted a white-frame building on the left with a blue and pink sign on it: Cozy Café. Attached to the café was the Cozy Bar, but it wasn't open yet. I decided to stop at the café, get a cup of coffee, and ask a few questions.

The aroma of strong coffee and grease greeted me as I

stepped inside. Two couples sat in pink booths with white-topped tables, but no one sat at the L-shaped counter. A man whose stained white apron barely reached around him was cooking eggs and bacon at the grill. A tall woman in a dark green dress stood near the cash register and eyed me. She was thin, from her figure to her face. Even her nose was thin. I crossed the black-and-white checkerboard tile floor to the counter and slid onto a stool. The pop of grease and the clatter of silverware on dishes filled the air.

The woman sauntered over. "You're not from around here," she stated as she primped her carefully curled hairdo with her pencil.

I nodded. "Is it that obvious?"

She smiled and gave me a knowing nod. "I know all the locals." She picked up a pad and poised her pencil over it. "What can I get you?"

"Just a cup of coffee." I took off my hat and set it on the counter.

"Sure thing." She plopped the pad and pencil down and poured me a hot cup of joe.

"Thanks." The coffee was steaming, so I let it sit for a minute. "Have you worked here long?"

"You could say that," she said. "Earl," she jerked a thumb at the cook, "and I grew up in town. There are times I think I'd like to move on, but..." she shrugged.

"I was hoping to find someone like you," I said, as a story formed in my mind.

She cocked an eyebrow at me. "Oh?"

"I'm an old family friend of the Norlands," I said. "I knew his daughters way back when and –"

"Ruby and Edith," she interrupted.

"That's right. I haven't seen them in ages, and since I was passing through town, I thought I might look them up."

"They haven't lived here for a few years," she said.

I tested the coffee. It was strong, the way I liked it. "I knew the family when they lived in Kansas, before they moved here."

"Oh, that was a long time ago," Earl said as he put two plates of eggs and bacon on the counter. "Here you go, Opal."

"Excuse me," Opal said. She picked up the plates and walked around the counter, then headed for one of the booths.

"I was a boy when I last saw them." I continued my ruse. "What happened to the girls?"

"Ruby was a teacher here in town," Earl said as he wiped big hands on his apron. "And the other girl, Edith, she married a guy she met in Denver, but he went off to the war and she came here to live with Ruby."

"They were out at the family place east of town," Opal said as she returned to her spot behind the counter. "It was their father's place and they moved in there when he died."

"Where's that?" I asked.

"Southeast of town," Opal repeated. "Off of Highway 287."

"Never saw Edith much, though," Earl muttered.

Opal nodded. "That's the truth."

I took a sip of coffee. "Why is that?"

She frowned. "Ruby said her sister was sickly and weak, so she stayed at the house."

"She didn't work at all?" I asked. Gordon Sandalwood had said that Edith worked at a grocery store for a while.

"Not when she first came to stay at Ruby's, but eventually she worked at the grocery store."

"The Piggly Wiggly?"

"That only opened a couple years ago," Earl said.

"It was the local market." Opal rested her hands on the counter and leaned down. "You ask me, I think she was pining for her husband. Him being off in the Pacific and a small town gal like her all alone in Denver. It had to be hard for her, so

Ruby brought her out here. It took about a year, but Edith finally perked up."

"I'm glad," I said.

"But Lester didn't help matters," Earl said. "That man could make anyone crazy."

"Lester?" I pretended I hadn't heard the name.

"Ruby's husband," Opal said. "I don't think he liked Edith at all, but he shouldn't have been talking. He's nothing but a no-account bum."

"Opal," Earl chided her.

She held up a hand. "He's nothing but a bum." Earl poured himself a cup of coffee, which looked tiny in his massive hands. He nursed it while he listened to Opal talk. "Those girls needed help on the farm," she said, "and he didn't do anything but drink and gamble. He'd come into the Cozy Bar and drink himself silly, then leave for days. There was some kind of trouble between him and Ruby, too, I don't know what, and then one day he up and left town. He'd show up, time to time, but that was just when he needed money."

"What a shame," I said.

"Yes." Opal nodded. "Those were such nice girls, too."

"Was Lester from around here?" I asked.

Opal nodded. "He grew up on a farm, too. I don't know what Ruby saw in him."

"I don't remember him," I said. "What's he look like?"

She shook her head. "He's thin, with dark hair."

"And he was tall," Earl interjected. "He was the basketball star in high school. Thought he had some potential..."

So not the brown-haired guy with a thin mustache, I thought.

"That boy never had any drive," Opal spat out. "Leaving those girls with the farm."

"Where did the girls move to?" I asked.

"Denver," they said in unison.

"Well, I'm on my way there, so I'll look them up," I said.

Opal smiled. "I'm sure they'd love some company."

"Say...do you know the Pattersons?"

Her eyebrow went up again. "Did they live around here?"

"I thought so," I said. "But my memory might not be right."

"Do you have a first name?"

"I don't recall." I shrugged sheepishly. "It was a long time ago."

She pursed her lips and thought long and hard. "I don't know of anyone around here by that name." She glanced at Earl.

"Never heard of them," he said. "You ought to check at the post office, they might know."

"Paul?" Opal called out. A man with a handlebar mustache who was sitting with a heavyset woman in one of the booths turned to look at her. "You ever heard of a family around here, name of Patterson?"

He shook his head slowly. "No, doesn't sound familiar." He looked at his wife and she shook her head in the same slow way he had. "No," he repeated.

Opal gestured at the couple at the other booth. They'd been listening and they both shrugged.

"Check the post office," Paul suggested.

Opal and Earl turned back to me.

"Good idea," I said.

"You sure they lived around here?" Opal asked.

"I thought so," I said. I finished my coffee, put some change on the counter and stood up. "Thanks for a great cup of coffee."

"Be careful driving to Denver," Opal said as she scooped up the coins.

I put on my hat and tapped the brim. "I will." I walked to the door, then stopped. "Where's the post office?"

41

"Go east and hang a right on B Avenue," Opal said. "You can't miss it."

I thanked her again and strolled out the door.

CHAPTER SEVEN

There was no wind today, but it was cold, with a chill that sank right through to your bones. The air had the smell of snow in it, and I hoped I wouldn't get caught in a storm out here on the plains. If that happened, the highway could be shut down, and I'd be stuck in Limon.

I hustled back to the Plymouth and drove to the post office. It was a small, unassuming building with a big front window. I went inside and waited while a woman holding a big package stood at the high counter and talked to a clerk with wispy gray hair.

"I don't understand why it's so much," the woman was saying.

"Well, Mrs. Saunders, it's because of the weight," the clerk said, his tone exceedingly patient.

"Yes, but there's not much in the box," she protested.

"Yes, I know," the clerk said. He then launched into a tedious explanation of shipping costs.

I shifted from foot to foot while they discussed the price, then looked around at the advertising posters on the wall. I finally glanced very impatiently at my watch. The woman at last wrapped up her business, and when she left, the clerk and I were by ourselves.

"Can I help you?" he asked in an eager voice, seemingly glad to have someone to talk to.

"I hope so," I said as I stepped up to the counter. He was short, like Napoleon, and he sat on a high stool. I didn't want to tower over him because I'd learned over the years that that could intimidate people, so I bent down and leaned against the counter. Now we were at eye level. Much friendlier. "I'm looking for the Pattersons. Opal at the café said I should check with you. Have you heard of them?"

"Patterson." His wizened face wrinkled up. "Can't say that I know the name, and I've been here a long time. And you don't have an address," he said, disappointment in his tone.

"No, I don't. I was told they might live around here."

"I know just about everybody in these parts." He put a gnarled hand to his chin and thought long and hard. "Hmm. Maybe let it percolate for a minute and it'll come to me."

"Did you know the Norlands?"

He smiled. "Yep. Knew John and the girls. And that fellow Lester that Ruby hooked up with." When he mentioned Lester, it was as if he had poison on his tongue. It seemed no one liked Lester. "They lived south of town. Old John was a doctor and he did some farming, too."

"And Ruby sold the place after John died?" I asked to keep him talking.

"Yep. It was hard on her, and she couldn't keep up the place after her father died. Once Ruby decided to move, she packed up pretty quick and left. I think she left a lot of stuff here, rather than move it to Denver."

"Has Lester been around lately?"

He scratched his chin. "Haven't seen him."

I was getting nowhere. "Anyone else I might talk to about the Pattersons?"

He blinked a few times, and then his eyes lit up. "Patterson, you say?"

I nodded.

"There might've been a couple that lived in Burlington for a short while," he said. "Ralph and Gladys."

"Burlington? That's almost to the state border."

"Yep."

"You're sure?" I pressed. I didn't relish driving almost to Kansas on what was seeming more and more like a wild goose chase.

"I seem to remember my wife talking about a Gladys Patterson that a friend of hers knew. Clarence at the post office in Burlington might know. Tell him Albert sent you."

"Thanks," I said. "I'll do that."

I turned for the door.

"Funny, two people asking about folks in the same week," he murmured.

I whirled around. "Excuse me?"

He stopped and stared at me as if he'd been caught telling a lie. "What?"

"Someone else was in here asking about the Pattersons?"

"Not the Pattersons. The Norlands."

"Who asked you about the Norlands?"

"Never seen him before."

"He didn't happen to have brown hair, a mustache, and a pork pie hat, did he?"

"No, that doesn't sound like him. This fellow wasn't very tall, but he was big, with dark, slicked-back hair. He wasn't very friendly."

"Why was he asking about the Norlands?"

He pointed out the window. "He wanted to know where

they lived. I told him the Hoffmans live there now." He blinked at me.

"That's it?"

"Yep."

I nodded slowly as I went out the door. When I got back to the Plymouth, I pulled my Rand McNally map out of the glove box and studied it. The old Norland place, which now belonged to the Hoffmans, was south on Highway 287. I could stop by there first and see if the Hoffmans knew anything about the Pattersons and this strange man with the slicked-back hair. Then I'd drive on to Burlington, which was almost eighty miles away.

I put the map on the passenger seat and drove east down Main Street, which curved south and turned into Highway 287. When I got to County Road 23, I turned right and followed the dirt road for a few miles as it meandered through the prairie. During the summer, the land on either side would be green with alfalfa, sugar beets, or some other crop, but now it was barren and dreary. I crossed Big Sandy Creek and drove slowly until I finally saw a lone turnoff. I stopped and peered down a long, narrow drive.

Off in the distance was a solitary two-story house. It was bright yellow, with a long front porch. Beyond the house were a barn, a chicken coop, and a small brick grain silo. I didn't see any vehicles in front of the house. I turned and crept up the drive and stopped in front of the house. I waited a few seconds and then got out. Chickens pecked near the coop, their clucks filling the crisp air, which carried a faint alfalfa odor.

I walked around the front of the Plymouth and up the porch steps. They creaked loudly. I reached the door, knocked and waited a moment, then knocked again. I wondered if the Hoffmans were gone. I tried the doorknob. Locked. Who locks their doors out in the country?

I walked over to a window next to the door and peeked into what was a small living room with faded floral wallpaper, a sofa, and two wingback chairs near a fireplace. I didn't see anyone. I tapped on the window and called out again, then strode to the end of the porch and listened. Nothing but the chickens. I stepped off the porch and walked across hard dirt toward the barn. As I neared it, I heard a faint moo. Then I noticed cows in a field behind the barn. I reached a fence that ran around the barn and called out again. A dog barked and a woman's voice scolded it.

I had started toward a gate when a large barn door flew open. A sturdy-looking woman in a print dress stood in the doorway. She glared at me with beady eyes, but I was watching the shotgun she had pointed at me.

"What do you want?" she snapped in a high-pitched voice that had a steel edge to it. A big German Shepherd sat at her heels. He snarled and his growling carried through the fence to me.

"Mrs. Hoffman?" I lifted my hands, palms up. "I want to ask a few questions, that's all." My stomach knotted as it had so many times during the war. You never get used to being on the wrong end of a weapon.

"Who are you?"

"I knew the previous owners," I said, keeping up the ruse I'd started at the café.

"The Norlands?" She took a couple of steps away from the barn door. Sunlight glinted off the barrel of the shotgun. She held it like she knew how to use it.

"That's right."

The beady eyes narrowed. "They haven't lived here for years."

"I know. Did you ever meet the girls, Edith and Ruby?"

"We talked to Ruby some, but I don't know Edith."

"I thought I might look around, for old time's sake."

"I don't think so," she said.

"Do you think you could put the gun away?" I asked as politely as I could.

She glared at me. "We've had people snooping around lately. I don't know what the sudden interest is in this house."

That explained the locked front door, and her greeting me with a shotgun. "Was it a gentleman with dark, slicked-back hair, kind of a big guy?" I asked.

"He wasn't a gentleman." She scowled at me. "You tell him we better not see him around here again, and he better not try prowling about at night anymore or he'll get shot."

"Ma'am, I don't know him."

"Makes no difference to me. He was pushy, and he wanted to look around, like you. Said he might be interested in some of the furniture and things that Ruby left here. I told him it was ours now. He got nasty, and my husband had to run him off."

"Did this man tell you his name?"

"No."

"Where was he from?"

"He didn't say." The shotgun wavered, but only because she used it to gesture at the road. "You need to leave now."

"Yes, ma'am." I turned and walked sideways, so I could still see her and the shotgun.

She walked to the gate and deftly opened it with one hand, the shotgun pressed tightly against her body with her other arm, but still aimed squarely at me. The dog trotted with her.

"Hurry up," she chided as she put the shotgun in both hands again.

I sped up. "Do you know the Pattersons?" I called over my shoulder.

"Never heard of them. You go on now, or I'll fire a shot that'll bring my husband in from the field."

Since the land around us was desolate, I doubted her husband was working in them. He was probably gone, and she was trying to bluff me. But there was no point in pushing her. I went around to the driver's side of the Plymouth and opened the door. The woman had reached the edge of the porch. She stood and watched me, the Shepherd still with her.

I tipped my hat at her. "Ma'am." I got in the car and drove slowly back down the drive, then glanced into the rearview mirror. Mrs. Hoffman had walked to the front of the house, the shotgun still aimed in my direction. As I turned onto the road, I wondered about this other guy that had her so spooked.

CHAPTER EIGHT

I hightailed it out of there and back to Highway 287. No one seemed to know the Pattersons. And what was it about the Norland house that had this other dark-haired stranger wanting to look around? Was this related to whatever Edith and Ruby were hiding?

I drove back into Limon and stopped at a Texaco to gas up. The attendant whistled as he worked the pump, and when he finished, he quickly wiped the front windshield.

"Want me to check the oil?" he asked.

"That's okay, Mac," I said. "Hey, do you know the Pattersons?"

"Don't think so."

I wasn't surprised.

He leaned on the car. "That'll be a two bucks."

He was curt, so I didn't ask him for any more information. I handed him a bill and drove off.

Almost two hours later, I arrived in Burlington. I knew little about the town, except that many years before, Elitch Gardens, one of Denver's amusement parks, had sold its carousel to Kit Carson County, and the carousel was now in Burlington. I remembered riding the old carousel as a kid and I'd marveled at the hand-carved and painted animals. The carousel had been a thing of beauty, but I'd heard it had fallen into disrepair.

Burlington was a small town, and I easily found the post office. But I didn't have high hopes that the clerk, Clarence, would know anything about the Pattersons. I parked on the street, got out, slammed my door and strolled into the building. It was similar to the one in Limon, a big room with a high counter, a wall of brass post office boxes, and the same advertising posters on the other walls. The only difference was the man behind the counter, who was a good twenty years younger than the guy in Limon.

The clerk was bustling around behind the counter, and when he heard the door open, he looked up and flashed a smile full of yellow teeth. "What can I do for you?"

I crossed to the counter and leaned against it. "Are you Clarence?"

"That's right." The smile remained.

"Albert at the post office in Limon said I should talk to you."

He placed pudgy hands on the counter. "All right, then, I'm listening."

"You wouldn't happen to know a family named Patterson from somewhere around here?" I was getting tired of hearing myself ask the question.

He nodded. "Yeah, I know of them. They lived east of town, kind of kept to themselves. They'd come in here once in a while for something. I think they moved here from Missouri."

"Really?" I shoved my hat back, stunned. Someone actually knew the Pattersons.

"Yes, but they moved away."

I went from being stunned to disappointed in a second. "Where'd they move to?"

"Vernon. I had to forward some mail to them."

I frowned. "Never heard of it."

"It's about forty miles north of here."

"How long ago did they move?"

"Oh, about seven or eight years ago. I don't remember for sure. I heard they bought an old farm outside of town."

"Do they still live there?"

"I don't know. I never knew them personally."

"How do I get to Vernon?"

"Take Highway 385 north to County Road 26. It's out in the middle of nowhere. Here, let me write it down." He grabbed a piece of paper and a pencil and jotted down the directions. "There's not much in Vernon, except they do have a nice school there for the kids in that area. That farm is west of Vernon. I don't remember the road, but you go south about two miles. Look for a farm on the west side of the road. It's the only one for miles."

I thanked him and left. I topped off the gas tank again, stopped at a local tavern for a ham sandwich and a cup of coffee, and then began the journey to Vernon. It took me over an hour to get to County Road 26, but it gave me time to think about what I'd say if I found the Pattersons. I couldn't very well tell them that I knew Edith and Ruby, since it appeared the Pattersons were in on whatever the girls were hiding. And the story of growing up in the area would only get me so far. So, how could I get the information I needed? Then something occurred to me. The country was due for another census the following year, so I could pretend to be a census taker. It wasn't likely the Pattersons would know exactly when someone would call on them about the census. And this ploy would allow me to ask them plenty of questions.

Once I'd made up my mind what to do, I fought off boredom. Eastern Colorado is flat and without a lot of character. I felt like I was the only man on earth as I passed empty fields that lost themselves in the horizon. I didn't see a single car until I neared Vernon, a tiny town with few streets. I stopped at the only store in town and asked for directions to the Patterson farm, and was told it was on County Road BB. I headed farther west, and ten minutes later found the county road. I turned south as I'd been told to do, and I finally came upon the Patterson place.

After my encounter with Mrs. Hoffman, I was wary. I parked at the end of the road and studied the house. It was a run-down single story that was in dire need of paint, but the windows were clean and the area around the house was tidy. A barn behind the house was weathered and gray. Two huge maple trees towered over the barn, nice shade in the summer, but bare now. Typical farm property in eastern Colorado. I didn't see a car or truck anywhere.

I watched for five minutes, and when nothing happened, I eased down the drive and approached the house. I parked in front and cautiously got out. I stood with the door open and listened. Only a cold stillness. Then a woman came around from the back of the house. She was a spindly woman in a long coat that was too big for her small frame. She had dark hair that fell around square shoulders. She held a basket of folded laundry in her hands, much less dangerous than a shotgun. She saw me, and a curious look crossed her face.

"Hello," she called out.

I shut the door and walked toward her.

"Is there something I can do for you?" she asked. Much more friendly than Mrs. Hoffman.

I smiled. "I hope so."

Just then, a boy who was about six ran around the corner of the house. He came up behind her and stared at me as he fiddled with buttons on his coat. And I suddenly knew what Edith and Ruby were hiding.

CHAPTER NINE

The boy was the spitting image of Edith Sandalwood. He had the same blond hair, dark eyes and round face. He pursed his lips at me, and it was like seeing Edith as she sat unhappily at the Rexall the other day while she talked to her sister Ruby.

"May I help you?" the woman repeated, her tone light and curious.

"Yes, ma'am," I said. "Are you Mrs. Patterson?"

"Yes. Call me Gladys."

"My name is Dewey Webb and I'm with the Census Bureau. If you have time, I'd like to ask you some questions."

"Why, yes. I didn't know the census was due."

"It's just getting started."

"Here, Gerry, take this." She handed the laundry basket to the boy, fiddled with her hair, and then smoothed her dress. She started for the front door. "Come on in."

Gerry hefted the basket with both hands and staggered after us into the house. We entered into a small kitchen with an old range, a sink with a pump, and a large oak table and four chairs. Faded wallpaper covered the walls, and the wood floors were rough. It was simple and clean.

She shrugged out of the coat and hung it on a peg near the door. "Gerry, take those clothes into my room, and then finish your chores."

"Yes, ma'am." He went through a door to the right with the basket, then reappeared empty-handed. He stared shyly at me for a second, then ran out the front door.

"May I offer you a cup of coffee?" Gladys asked.

"That would be nice."

She gestured at a chair. "Sit over here near the heater, where it's warmer."

I took a seat where she'd indicated, by a cast-iron space heater, and relished the warmth. I took off my hat and rested it on my knee. Some papers, a bag of tobacco and rolling paper, and some yarn were on the table. She moved them aside, poured coffee from a pot on the stove and set it down in front of me.

"Thank you," I said. "It gets mighty cold out here on the plains."

"Yes, it does." She sat down opposite me, took a shawl from the chair back, and wrapped it around herself, then waited.

I took a sip of the coffee. Weak and bitter. It'd probably been sitting for a while. I took a notebook and pen out of my coat pocket and pretended to be official.

"Now," I said, then smiled at her. "Your full name?"

"Gladys Catherine Patterson."

I wrote it down. "And the address here is..."

She told me and I added it to the notepad. I'd been a much younger man the only time I'd had to answer any census questions, but I did my best to remember what they were.

"How long have you lived here?" I began.

"About eight years."

I feigned interest. "And you moved here from?"

"Limon."

"I see." I noted that. "And there is a head of household?"

"My husband, Ralph."

"Is he here now?"

She shook her head. "He had to go into Burlington for feed."

"And Ralph's only work is this farm?"

"Yes, that's correct."

"Do you work?"

"No."

"How much money did your husband make from the farm last year?"

"I don't know for sure. We get by."

I glanced around at the sparse surroundings. They were getting by, but I suspected just barely.

"We'll check with your husband later." I took another sip of coffee and continued. "How many children do you have?"

"Just Gerry." She spelled the name for me.

"He must be about six or seven?"

"He's six," she said.

I nodded. "So he was born in Limon?"

"Yes, I mean, uh...no, he was born in Nebraska."

"Nebraska?"

"Yes, he –"

The door burst open and Gerry ran into the kitchen. "Mother, what can I do now?" he interrupted.

Gladys leaped to her feet, startled. "Aren't you doing your chores?"

"I finished," he said.

"Is there ice in the water trough?" she asked.

He pouted. "I didn't check."

"Go do that, and make sure the stalls in the barn are cleaned out."

"But, Mother, that's not part of my chores."

"Do it," she said, her tone stern.

"Yes, ma'am." Gerry turned and plodded out the door.

Gladys moved over to a window and peered out. Then she looked back at me. "What were you saying?"

"Gerry was born in Nebraska?" I asked.

"Yes."

"And you're his mother?"

An almost imperceptible hesitation. "Yes."

She was lying. And she knew that I knew it. Her eyes held fear. I waited, careful not to press too much. I didn't want her getting suspicious and kicking me out.

"His momma got into some trouble," she finally said in a small voice, "but she couldn't care for him, so we took him in. We never officially adopted him." She glanced out the window again, then at me. "He doesn't know."

"I see."

"This," she gestured at my notepad, "doesn't need to be reported, does it?"

I had no idea what the government would do, but I had the information I wanted. "I'll note he was born here."

She let out a relieved breath. "Thank you."

I asked a few more questions, then put the notepad and pen away. "I think I have everything for now. Someone will be around to follow up with a few more questions for your husband, just routine." I stood up and put on my hat.

"I'll let him know to expect it."

"Thank you for the coffee."

"My pleasure," she said hurriedly. She was ready for me to leave.

She followed me outside and watched as I got in the Plymouth, then waved as I drove off. I circled back through Vernon to County Road 26. The sun was low in the sky, and it created a glare as I turned south, but by the time I reached Limon, dusk had settled in, along with a light but steady snow.

I gassed up again, and then decided to stop in at the Cozy Bar for a drink. I'd been driving a lot today, and I wanted to see if the snow would pass. I didn't want to start back to Denver and get caught in the middle of nowhere during a storm.

When I walked into the bar, a jukebox was playing "Lovesick Blues," the only Hank Williams song I knew. A long wooden bar was near the back wall and some cowboys in leather boots and hats sat on barstools, drinking and talking. When the door opened, they turned and eyed me, the stranger, carefully. I stepped up to the bar.

"Scotch," I said to the bartender.

He studied me with inquisitive eyes. "Passin' through?"

"Going to Denver, but I'm not sure about this weather."

"Supposed to get a few inches. Not much, but it can blow out there on the highway."

"I should probably stay here for the night."

"There's a good motel down the street," he said. He put a shot of Scotch down in front of me.

I downed it, then gestured for another. He poured it and I paid him, nodded at the cowboys, and took my drink to a booth in the corner, where I could look out the window at the falling snow. I hadn't planned to spend the night, and I was feeling sore. I'd rather go home and be with my wife and son. I nursed my Scotch, lit a cigarette, and thought about Clara. We'd only been married two years, but it seemed longer. I'd come home from the war with dark memories I couldn't seem to shake, but she'd helped me start to escape them. She had her own painful past as well. Even though she hadn't served in the war, she'd suffered her own pain and loss when her fiancé hadn't returned. We'd felt that pain in each other, and through each other, we'd seen a way out of it.

Then my thoughts turned to Edith and a scenario formed in my mind. She'd married Gordon Sandalwood, and he'd immediately gone off to war. Then she'd met someone else and had gotten pregnant. Rather than tell her husband about her affair and baby, she'd gone to live with Ruby. She stayed out of sight until she had the baby, then gave him to the Pattersons, who seemed willing to keep her secret. So, I wondered, was the man in the pork pie hat blackmailing Edith, threatening to inform her husband about her son if she didn't pay up? That seemed like an easy bet.

Outside the window, wind whipped light snowflakes around and I pondered what to do next. I had a lot of questions for Edith. Had she wanted to give up her baby? Had Ruby forced her to? Who was the baby's father? Could he be blackmailing her? I shook my head in disgust. I couldn't answer those questions until I got back to Denver, which wasn't going to happen tonight.

I brooded for a bit longer, then downed the last of my Scotch, crushed out my cigarette, and walked out the door. I found the motel farther down on Main Street, paid for a room, and then used a pay phone to call Clara.

"Hello," she answered, her voice cheery.

"It's me. I'm stuck in Limon," I said.

"Oh?"

I explained about the snow.

"We had a dusting here, but it's gone."

"The storm's here now."

"I'll miss you, but you're better off not driving tonight," she said. "Is everything going okay?"

"Would you ever..."

"What?"

I hesitated. "Do you ever think about other men?"

"Dewey!" she said. "What's this about?"

"Ah, I don't know."

"Sweetheart, there's only you."

"Yeah."

"Is this about a case?"

"I can't put anything past you."

"You can talk to me about it, if you want."

I shook my head as if she could see me. "It's nothing," I finally said.

I didn't usually talk business with Clara, so I changed the subject, and we chatted for a few minutes about her day, and about Sam before we hung up. Then I took the paper out of my wallet with Gordon Sandalwood's home phone number. I fed more coins into the slot and called him.

His greeting was gruff, but he turned eager when he realized who it was.

"What'd you find out?" he asked in a low voice.

"Not a whole lot," I said evasively. I wanted to talk to Edith before I shared anything with him. I figured I'd tell her what I knew, and let Edith tell her husband about her affair. Better he should hear it from her rather than me. And then, if she was being blackmailed, I could help them, if they wanted me too. "Give me another day or two to see what I can turn up."

"Take whatever time you need," he said.

"I'll be in touch."

I hung up and went to my room. And then I remembered Opal from the café, and Mrs. Hoffman mentioning the dark-haired fellow who was poking around Limon. He wasn't the same man Edith had met in the park. Who was he, and was he still in Limon?

I peeked out the window to the parking lot. A few other

cars were parked there along with my Plymouth. I locked the room door and checked my gun before I went to bed.

CHAPTER TEN

The storm passed during the night, and the sun was already melting the snow when I left the motel. I wanted to avoid Opal and Earl, for fear that they'd ask me why I was still in town, or that they'd poke holes in my story about knowing Edith and Ruby. So I grabbed breakfast at a different café, and then drove back to Denver.

I arrived just after ten and stopped at my office, which was two rooms on the second floor of the old Victorian. The outer office served as a waiting room, with a small couch and a desk for a secretary. I didn't make enough money to afford anyone, but I kept a typewriter and phone there, so it looked professional. An accountant had an office at the other end of the hall, and his secretary could see my door. If she saw that I had visitors, she'd take a message and slip a note under my door.

The inner office wasn't much bigger than the waiting room. I'd furnished it with an old oak desk, a small leather couch, two club chairs across from my desk, and a file cabinet in the corner. Nothing hung on the walls, and the only personal item was a picture of Clara that sat on the desk. It faced east and the sunlight that came through the window warmed an otherwise chilly room. It wasn't much, but since I wasn't there often, it was all I needed.

I took care of some paperwork, and then called Clara to let her know I was back in town and that I'd be home later in the day. Then I dialed Sandalwood's office to make sure he wasn't home with Edith.

"Sandalwood," he barked into the phone.

Good. That confirmed that he was at his office. I hung up quickly and dialed his home phone number.

"Hello?" Edith's silky voice said.

She was home. I hung up again, donned my hat, and headed to the Sandalwood house. If my luck stayed true, she would still be there by the time I arrived.

———

Twenty minutes later, I was standing on the Sandalwood front porch. The street was quiet as I rang the bell and waited. A moment later, Edith opened the door.

"Mrs. Sandalwood?" I asked.

"Yes?" she said. She wore a bright blue dress and her hair was perfectly coiffed, but her face was drawn with worry.

I went for the blunt approach. "You're in some trouble."

"Wha –" she stammered. "Who are you?"

"My name is Dewey Webb. I'm a private detective." I took out my wallet and showed her my license. "Your husband hired me to follow you."

"Why, I...whatever for?" She was trying for cool and collected, but she was stumbling over herself. "I don't know what you're talking about."

I gave her a hard look. "He thinks something's going on with you, and he's right."

She wrung her hands, then glanced out into the street, worried that someone might see us talking. "You better come inside."

I followed her into a living room with a white tufted sofa and two armchairs, maple coffee table and end tables, and a floor-model Zenith radio that was playing jazz. The walls were covered in striped wallpaper and a fireplace in the corner had ashes and the remnants of a burned log in it. It would've been cozy, if not for the tension thick in the air. She sat on the edge of the sofa, then gestured for me to sit in the armchair.

"What do you think is going on?" Her voice was strained.

Good move on her part, to see what I knew, and then she could cover for herself.

"I saw you meet a guy in the park last Friday," I countered.

"Oh, that." She gestured dismissively. "I got myself into a bit of money trouble, and that was a friend of mine. I was paying him back." Straight for the lie.

"I also overheard you talking to your sister about the Pattersons."

"Who?"

I locked eyes with her. "I've been to Vernon."

"Where's that?"

"I found the Pattersons."

Her mouth opened, but no words came out.

"I saw your son."

A hand flew to her face. "The Pattersons told you?"

I shook my head. "No, Mrs. Patterson lied for you, but it was easy to see that Gerry wasn't her son. He looks just like you."

Something akin to hope flashed in her eyes. "They named him Gerry?"

"Yes."

"And he's okay?"

"He's fine, as far as I could tell."

She smiled faintly, then drew in a breath and let it out slowly. "I haven't seen him since the day he was born –" She choked up, then leaped to her feet. "Excuse me." She ran into the kitchen. Through the doorway, I could see her standing near the sink, her body wracked with sobs. She finally gathered herself and came back into the living room. "I'm sorry."

"No need to apologize," I said. "It must've been difficult for you."

"It was." She sat down and smoothed her dress, and then her words tumbled out as she shared the whole story with me. "I'd barely known Gordon before he went off to war. It was a whirlwind romance, and then there I was all by myself in this big city. I got a job at Lowry Air Force Base, and there was an Army Air Force fellow who saw me eating alone at lunch. He asked me one day why I wasn't eating with the other girls, and I couldn't explain why exactly, just that I didn't fit in with the girls, and that I was lonely. After that, he and I ate lunch together. Then lunch became dinner, and one thing led to another. I suddenly realized I was in love with him, and not Gordon. And I thought this man loved me. Then I found out I was pregnant, and when I told him, I thought I would leave Gordon to be with him. Only he," she hesitated, then sniffled and said, "not only did he not want me, I found out he was married. He was furious and said he never wanted to see me again. I was devastated, and I didn't know what to do. I was embarrassed that I'd been so foolish, and I just couldn't tell Gordon. He'd been so sweet, sending me letters from overseas, and here I was, being unfaithful to him. I told my sister, Ruby, and we decided that I would move out to Limon. She knew the Pattersons, and knew they wanted to have children but couldn't. She arranged for them to take the baby and move somewhere else."

"So you had the baby and let the Pattersons take him, and no one was the wiser," I said.

"Yes."

"Or so you thought."

A lone tear streaked down her cheek. "I don't know what I'm going to do."

I leaned forward and rested my elbows on my knees. I tried to soften my tone. "Why not tell Gordon?"

"I can't. He'd be devastated, and I don't want to do that to him. I've grown to love him, and I don't want him to know about this." She threw me a pleading look. "Please don't tell him."

"He said," I hesitated to bring up a delicate subject, "you can't have children."

She sighed. "I haven't been able to get pregnant since then. I don't know why."

"You're being blackmailed, correct?"

"Yes."

"And the man you met in the park wants money or he's threatening to tell Gordon about your indiscretions."

"There was only one," she said indignantly.

I frowned. "It was enough, wasn't it?"

"Yes," she said miserably.

"Tell me about the blackmailing."

Her eyes lowered as she thought about it. "I received a note about two weeks ago, a few days before Thanksgiving. I read it so many times, I have it memorized. It said 'We want one thousand dollars or we will tell Gordon about your affair.' Then it gave directions to go to City Park at noon on December 2nd and wait at the bench south of the Pavilion."

A thousand dollars. That was a lot of money.

"Who's *we*?" I asked.

She shrugged. "I don't know."

"Did more than one person meet you?"

"No, it's been the same man both times."

"And you don't know him."

"I've never seen him before in my life."

"Did he give you a name?"

"No. When I asked him why he was doing this, he said he was just the middleman. I asked him if he delivered the note to my house, and he denied it."

"Where's the note now?"

"I burned it, so Gordon wouldn't find it."

"And let me guess," I said. "You didn't have all the money."

"Not anywhere close. I save a little here and there, leftovers from my shopping money. I usually use it to buy gifts for Gordon. It amounted to almost a hundred dollars. Not nearly enough. I spent this whole time trying to find some odd jobs, and I even tried to figure out who that man in the park was." She gave a little shake of her head. "I didn't have any luck."

"And that's why you've been coming home late, or why you're not around when Gordon calls."

She sucked in a nervous breath and nodded. "He's noticed I haven't been myself."

"Yeah. That's why he hired me, remember?"

She took a few more deep breaths, then continued. "Anyway, the other day, I took what money I had to that man, and he said it wasn't the right amount. I told him I didn't have any more, and I begged him to let that be enough, but he said he didn't have any say in it."

I remembered her in the park, clutching at the man's arm. "And he gave you until tomorrow to come up with the rest."

"Yes."

"It sounds like this man, or whoever he's working with, knew you might not have had time to come up with it all, and he was prepared to give you more time."

"I suppose."

"They've thought this through," I said. "The note you received, was it handwritten or typed?"

"Typed. That was one of my errands. I took it to a type-writer repair shop. The owner said the note was typed on a Corona. Not that that helped me."

"How was it delivered? Through the post?"

She shook her head. "No. Someone stuck it to the door, then rang the bell and left."

"Whoever delivered it knew that Gordon was at work and only you would get it."

"I hadn't thought of that."

"And you're going to pay him?"

"What choice do I have? I'll give him the rest, but what will I do if he wants more?" She stood up and began to pace.

"That's a possibility," I said. "Do you have any idea who's blackmailing you?"

"I don't know."

"Who knew about the baby, besides the father, Ruby, and the Pattersons?"

"No one."

"Who's the father?"

She shook her head vehemently. "It doesn't matter now."

"Mrs. Sandalwood," I began.

"I'm not telling you his name."

I sighed. "What about Lester? Was he around?" She stopped pacing and stared at me. I shrugged. "I know about him, too."

She raised her eyebrows. "You really do know everything, don't you?"

"I don't know who's blackmailing you."

"Neither do I." She sighed. "Anyway, Ruby was still with Lester when I lived out there, but he was hardly ever around."

"But he knew you were pregnant."

"Yes, but he swore he wouldn't tell anybody."

"Can you believe him?"

"I..." Her voice trailed off.

I sat back. "We have at least a few people who could be blackmailing you." I ticked them off on my hand. "The father, the Pattersons, and Lester."

"None of them would do this to me."

"How can you be sure?"

She didn't say anything for a moment. "But I don't know the man who met me in the park."

"It sounds like he may have been hired," I said. "And anyone who *did* know about the baby could've told others about you."

She turned white. "I don't think so." There was little conviction in the statement. She took another deep breath. "Can you find who's doing this? Please."

I didn't answer for a long minute. "If I find who it is, what will you tell Gordon? He knows something isn't right with you."

"I'll think of something. Will you help me?" Her eyes were pleading.

I'd come here thinking I'd convince Edith to talk to her husband about her affair. But now it appeared I was going to be helping her without Gordon knowing.

I leaned back in my chair. "Let's talk about your next meeting with this blackmailer," I said.

CHAPTER ELEVEN

Thursday the sun was out, and it was warmer than it had been in a week. A little before noon, I was in City Park, sitting in the Plymouth. I had parked where I could see the spot where Edith would meet her blackmailer. Yesterday, after she'd told me her story and I'd decided to help her, we'd discussed her next meeting with the man in the pork pie hat. Since I didn't need to follow her, I could wait in the park, watch for him, and follow him when he left the park.

At ten minutes before twelve, Edith drove by me in her blue Chrysler. She parked in the same place she had the previous Friday, got out, and hurried to the bench near the grove of maple trees. I'd instructed her not to look around for me, and so she sat on the bench and stared straight ahead.

Right at noon, the blackmailer emerged from behind the Pavilion, crossed the road, and walked through the trees to Edith. I watched through binoculars as he stopped in front of her, not bothering to sit down. She handed him an envelope. He glanced inside it, then said something to her, and Edith nodded. He said something else and she threw up her hands and then wept. She talked for a moment and the guy shrugged, said something else, and then turned and stomped away.

I wanted to know what he'd said to Edith, but it would have to wait. The man had parked somewhere on the north side of the Pavilion, so I followed the road as it meandered around the building. The road forked and I turned right, then drove until I came to a parking lot. I pulled into a space and waited. A minute later, the man appeared near the building and walked to an old jalopy that had seen better days. He got in, squealed out of the lot, and zoomed to the west. I counted to five, then quickly followed. He reached York Street and headed south to Eighteenth, then west through downtown.

The jalopy eventually turned onto Lipan Street, an area of town I wouldn't want to live in. It was known for unsavory characters who lived hard, with rows of old two-story apartment buildings. The car flew down the street and screeched to a halt in front of a building with dirty windows and worn white siding. My quarry got out of the car, tossed a cigarette into the gutter, then walked up a cracked sidewalk and disappeared into the building.

I drove down the block until I found a spot to leave the Plymouth, then raced back to the building and went inside. A tiny foyer was dimly lit with a single bulb. A musty, stale odor assaulted my nostrils. I coughed and glanced around. Directly in front of me were stairs. To my left was a long hallway, and right by the entrance were mail slots with labels on them. I stood for a moment and listened. The sound of Bing Crosby crooning filtered through another door at the bottom of the stairs. Other than that, nothing. The man in the pork pie hat had vanished.

I strolled down the hallway and listened at the doors to two apartments. Silence. I came back to the stairs and put my ear to the door by the entrance. I couldn't hear anything but Bing. I looked up the stairs, then tiptoed up to the second floor. There were three apartment doors up here. I stood quietly for a moment by each one, but was again disappointed to hear nothing. I slipped back downstairs and stopped at the mailboxes. The box for each unit was labeled with a last name, but none of them meant anything to me. I was pondering what to do next when the door by the stairs opened. Bing crooned even louder. I whirled around to see a wrinkled old woman staring at me through thick glasses.

"Oh, I thought you might be the mailman," she said eagerly. Her pink housecoat may have fit at one time, but now it hung loosely on her frail frame.

I tipped my hat. "Sorry, wrong man." I poured on the charm, knowing she was exactly who I wanted to talk to, a woman whose wait for the postman was the most exciting part of her day. She'd want to chat.

She scrutinized me through the glasses. "You looking for a place to rent? I got one apartment available."

"You own the building?" I asked.

"I manage it. It pays for my place."

"I'm looking for someone," I said. "A guy with a pork pie hat and a black coat?"

"That's Sonny O'Hara." She glanced up the stairs and shuddered. "He lives up there, on the left." She squinted at me. "Are you friends with him?" The disapproval was clear in her voice.

"I'm a private detective," I said and showed her my license.

She snorted. "That figures."

"It does?"

She pulled her housecoat tight around her neck, then eyed the stairs again. "Come inside," she said in a low voice. She backed through her door and gestured for me to follow her.

The apartment was larger than I expected, with a sitting area, kitchen, and what I assumed was a bedroom at the back. The furniture was old, in a style that had gone stale twenty

75

years earlier. A faint odor of onions permeated the air. She went to a threadbare chair that sat next to an old radio perched on a crate. She eased into the chair, then turned down the music. I took a seat at the couch.

"You be careful around Sonny," she said.

I took off my hat and held it in my hands. "Why is that?"

"He's bad news." I waited. "This isn't the best neighborhood," she continued as she waved a hand to encompass the entire building. "Most folks work hard and try to be decent. But not Sonny. He's in with a bad crowd."

"Have you ever seen him with a guy who's stocky, with dark, slicked-back hair?" I asked, repeating the description provided by both Albert at the post office in Limon and Mrs. Hoffman.

Her lips moved in and out as she thought about it. "Yeah, that sounds like the fellow Sonny was with."

"Do you know his name?"

"Nothing comes to mind." She pointed a bony finger at me. "What's that boy up to?"

"That's what I'm trying to find out," I said.

"Something's been going on lately. He's been in and out at odd hours, and then there's that other fellow."

"What other fellow? The dark-haired man?"

She nodded, then eyed the ceiling, as if Sonny might hear her. She leaned forward. "I had the door open the other day, waiting for the mailman. Sonny and that other man came in, and I heard them talking. That fellow said something about getting him, and taking care of it." Her eyes darted up to the ceiling again. "He didn't sound nice about it."

"Taking care of what?" I mused.

"I don't know."

I glanced at the ceiling. "Did Sonny and this other man see you?"

"No, thank goodness. I stood behind the door. On their way

upstairs, Sonny talked about how much it was worth. And the other fellow said he 'had it at the house, and some of it might still be there.' Then Sonny asked who was going to go check. That's all I heard."

She struck me as a little hard of hearing, but she seemed pretty clear in her recollection of the conversation. I wondered how accurate it was.

"Did you see this man clearly?"

"He was like you say, with that hair slicked back with grease. I don't know who he was, but he looked mean." She shuddered at the recollection.

"Has he been around again?"

"No, that's the only time I saw him, and I hope he never comes back." She shivered again. "He's no good. But then, there's a couple of bad eggs around here. The man down the hall has a gambling problem. Why, just the other day –"

"Did you ever hear Sonny talk about Edith Sandalwood?" I interrupted.

She worked her lips again, in and out. "No, I don't recall that name."

"What does Sonny do for work?"

"Nothing steady, I can tell you that. I think he finds odd jobs here and there. He gets into too much trouble to keep a steady job."

"Is he behind on his rent?"

"No, always pays on time."

"So he's getting money from somewhere."

"Probably steals it," she said.

She was right about that, but I didn't say so. "Has Sonny ever been to jail?"

"I think so, but he's never told me. But he disappears for days at a time."

"There's no crime in that."

"That boy's been in jail, trust me." She nodded knowingly. "His type wasn't raised right, if you ask me. Now, back in my day –"

I stood up. "Thanks for your time. I'll show myself out." I'd gotten all I was going to get from her right now.

"You don't need to leave so soon," she said, a little too desperately. She needed the company, but I didn't have the time.

"I trust you'll keep this conversation between us," I said, throwing her a stern look.

"Of course," she said agreeably. As I put on my hat, she pushed herself out of the chair. "I'll walk you to the door." Anything for a little more conversation.

I thanked her again and stepped into the hallway. I waited for her to shut the door. Only, nosy parker that she was, she stood in the doorway and peered at me through her glasses. I nodded at her and slowly climbed the stairs, but I was hesitant. I wasn't afraid of Sonny; I'd easily handled punks like him. But Sonny was only a pawn in whatever was going on, and I wasn't ready to let him know someone was after him. I reached the top of the stairs and slipped around the corner, then paused. The landlady was still in her doorway, which irritated me. Whether I talked to Sonny or not was none of her business. I waited, and the landlady finally shut her door. The muffled sound of music began again.

I slipped down the hall to Sonny's door and listened. The dull hum of voices emanated through the cracks around the door, but I couldn't make out anything. I thought I heard footsteps approach the door, so I hurried back to the stairs and quietly tiptoed down to the ground floor and out the front door. I jogged back to the Plymouth and watched the building for a while, but Sonny never came out. I wanted to talk to Edith again before Sandalwood came home from work, so at three, I decided to leave. I knew where to find Sonny again. I remembered seeing a Conoco gas station on Colfax, so I headed there and called Edith from a pay phone.

"Oh, Mr. Webb!" she said breathlessly when I identified myself. "That man asked for more money!"

"How much more?" I asked.

"Ten thousand dollars. I told him I can't get that kind of money, and he said that wasn't his problem, that I'd better come up with it."

"How long did he give you to get the money?"

"A week."

"Then I have that long to find out who's behind this," I said. "Can you meet me at the Rexall in twenty minutes?"

"Yes, but why?"

"We need to talk, and you don't want your neighbors to see me at your house."

"Yes, that's good thinking. I'll leave right now."

"Good." I hung up and drove to the Rexall.

CHAPTER TWELVE

When I walked into the Rexall, Edith was sitting at the end of the lunch counter. She hadn't taken off her overcoat, and her purse was still slung over her shoulder. I sat on a stool next to her. She had both hands wrapped around a white coffee cup. I signaled the same baldheaded guy for coffee, then turned to her.

"I'm in trouble," she whispered. Her hand shook as she took a sip of coffee.

I tipped the brim of my hat up. "Tell me exactly what that man said to you when you gave him the money."

She thought for a second. "He asked if it was all there, and I said it was. Then he said I needed to come up with more. I started to argue with him and he said..." She closed her eyes as if picturing the scene. " 'Listen, doll, you gotta get the money or we'll tell your husband about the baby. You got a week.' I asked how he knew about the baby and he laughed. Then I said how in the world could I get that kind of money and he laughed again and said that it was my problem. Then he walked away." Her lower lip trembled and she dug into her purse for a handkerchief. She dabbed at her eyes, then drew in a breath and composed herself. "How am I going to come up with that kind of money?"

"This man obviously thinks you can, or he wouldn't be putting the screws to you like this," I said. The guy behind the counter returned with my coffee. I sipped some and waited for him to move down the counter and out of earshot. "Does the name Sonny O'Hara mean anything to you?"

"No," she said. "Should it?"

"He's the guy who's hustling you."

She stared at me. "How'd you find that out?"

I told her about my conversation with O'Hara's landlady.

"But how does he know about me and," she lowered her voice, "the baby? I don't know him."

"He must know someone who *does* know about you," I said. "O'Hara's been seen lately with another guy, stocky and slicked-back dark hair. Does he sound like anyone you know?"

She started to drink her coffee, then set her cup down with a loud clink. Coffee spilled on her hand, but she didn't notice. "No, I don't know him, either. Oh, this is so infuriating!"

I handed her a napkin, and then she noticed the spilled coffee. "You need to tell me about the man you had the affair with." I didn't mince any words. She started to protest, but I held up a hand to stop her. "If you want my help, it's time to name him. He might be behind this, or he might've told someone."

"No, he wouldn't have." She finally wiped off her hand and tossed the napkin in the cup.

"Mrs. Sandalwood," I scolded her.

She looked all around evasively and fiddled with the hand-kerchief. I looked, too. The drugstore was busy, with people rushing in, others leaving with bags. Outside the window, it was growing dark. A woman in red got out of a brand-new white

Cadillac. On the other side of the parking lot, a man in a dark fedora sat in a Mercury with a bent bumper. I saw an orange glow through the windshield. He was smoking a cigarette. Behind him, on Otis Street, two boys kicked a can down the sidewalk. I looked back at Edith. Her eyes finally alighted on me.

"The man's name was Fred Cooper," she said. "He was an officer in the Army Air Force. He was stationed at Lowry Air Force Base when I met him, and he lived near the base, but I don't know where he is now. He didn't want anything to do with me, and I was so hurt and devastated, I never wanted to see him again."

"What can you tell me about him?" I asked. "Is he still in the military?"

"Probably. He was looking to get promoted. But would he still be out at Lowry?"

"He could've transferred somewhere else and then back to Lowry." I thought about that, then said, "Where was he from, how old was he, that kind of thing?"

"He was from California, and he was in his late twenties when I met him. He has blond hair and dark eyes." She smiled faintly, and then it was gone. "Oh, he was handsome in his uniform, and he seemed so kind. He wasn't afraid to spend money on me." Hope sprang into her face. "He didn't need money then, so why would he be trying to get it from me now?"

The man had gotten her pregnant and then dumped her, and she still wanted to protect him.

"Things can change," I said. "Maybe he's in trouble now and needs money."

"He wouldn't blackmail me." The hope had faded just as quickly, and she said it without conviction.

"Maybe. He also could've told someone else."

"Fred wouldn't have said anything," she said. "He was

83

married, and he would've wanted to keep it quiet."

"You haven't had any contact with him since you told him about the baby?"

"Of course not."

"Then how do you know that he's still married, or that he hasn't ended up with money trouble?" I asked. "Or that he didn't tell someone else about you, and that person is black-mailing you."

She sighed heavily. "I guess any of that's possible."

"And the same could be said about Lester," I said. "So I need to find him, too."

She snorted. "Good luck. He hasn't been around in more than a year."

"Did he come to see you?"

"I was over at Ruby's one night, and he showed up. He'd cleaned himself up and had brought flowers. He told Ruby he wanted to get back together, that he'd changed, but I didn't believe him."

"Did Ruby?"

"No. She told him to leave and not come back. He got mad and threw the flowers at her, then walked off down the street, hollering that she was going to get what was coming to her."

"Has he tried to hurt her?"

Her eyes watered and she dabbed at them again. "Sometimes."

"Is she afraid he'll come back now?"

"Probably."

"But he hasn't been back since then?"

"Ruby hasn't mentioned it. You should be asking her about him."

"I will," I said, then gulped the last of my coffee and lit a cigarette. "But Ruby might try to sugarcoat things with me. I want your impression of him."

"He was a bum. I don't know what Ruby saw in him."

Two women carrying large bags sat down near us. I turned my back to them, so they wouldn't hear us talking.

"You said you never saw the Pattersons."

"Right."

'How do you know that they don't need the money?" I said. "From what I saw, any little bit would help."

She shook her head. "Ruby said they could be trusted."

"Maybe *they* told someone else about you."

"Why would anyone want to do this to me?" she said.

"That's the big question." I tapped the counter. "I need to talk to Ruby about them, and about Lester." I took out a nickel and slid it across the counter toward Edith. "Call your sister and tell her I'm coming over."

Edith hesitated.

I narrowed my eyes. "You haven't told her about me?"

She shook her head. "I thought maybe I could take care of this without her."

I took a drag off my cigarette, blew smoke, and said, "It's time to tell her now."

She stared at the nickel, then finally picked it up, slid off her stool, and went to the pay phone near the front door. I watched as she fed the money into the phone, dialed a number and talked for a minute, one hand clutching her handkerchief tightly. She did not look happy as she walked back to the lunch counter.

"She'll be home waiting for you," she said. "She asked if we can trust you."

I shrugged. "Do you have any other choice?"

She stared at her hands. "No."

"Where does she live?" I asked. Edith gave me the address. It was within ten minutes of my house.

We sat in silence for a minute. I stared out the window

again as I smoked. Shoppers came and went. The man in the fedora was still sitting in the Mercury. I squinted to get a better look at him.

"How are you going to find Fred?" she asked.

"I'll figure it out." I watched a woman cross the parking lot toward the Mercury, but she got into the car next to it. I studied the man in the fedora. "Turn around slowly," I said to Edith.

"What?" She whirled around and looked down at her dress. "Is there something on me?"

"There's a man who's been sitting in his car while we've been talking. He's in the Mercury. Don't look right at him."

Edith hesitated, then looked out the window.

"See him?" I asked. "In the fedora."

"Yes, but I can barely see him."

"Do you recognize the car?"

She shook her head, then turned back around. "What's going on?"

"It's probably nothing," I said. I stood up and crushed out my cigarette in an ashtray. "Let me walk you to your car."

She put her handkerchief back in her purse, and I paid for the coffee. Then we strolled outside. Darkness had settled in and I couldn't see into the Mercury. We walked to Edith's car, on the opposite side of the lot from the Mercury.

"I'll be in touch," I said, then waved her off.

As I walked back to my car, Edith drove out of the lot and headed east. The Mercury started up and went in the same direction. I fired up the Plymouth and screeched onto Colfax and followed the Mercury. It stayed on Colfax and kept pace with Edith's Chrysler, but then it turned on Sheridan. I thought he'd been after Edith, but I was wrong. I turned around at the next block. It was time to pay Ruby a visit.

CHAPTER THIRTEEN

Ruby Klassen lived on Fox Street in the Baker neighborhood, where the houses had gone up at the turn of the century. They varied in style from two-story Victorians to plain bungalows and duplexes. The houses on Fox were all tiny and single-story, some with siding, but most constructed of brick, and all built so close to each other that a man could barely walk between them. Maple and oak trees towered over the street, their barren branches skeletal at this time of the year. Ruby's house was long and narrow, with brown siding and white trim, a small front porch, and a sliver of lawn. Dead leaves littered the gutters and street, but the area around Ruby's house had been swept clean. I parked across the street and strolled up to the front door. Before I could knock, the door opened to reveal Ruby, with a frown on her face. She was in a flowered dress, but she'd traded heels for slippers.

"You're Dewey Webb." It was a pronouncement more than a question.

"Yes, ma'am." I took off my hat at her.

She glanced up and down the street. "You'd better come in," she finally said.

I followed her into a minuscule living room that had a small loveseat and an overstuffed chair, both covered in green fabric. A radio sat on a table in the corner, but it wasn't on. She gestured at the loveseat without offering me anything to drink, then settled down into the chair with a sigh.

"By the end of the day, I just want to sit for a bit," she said.

"You're a teacher?" I asked as I sat down and put my hat beside me.

"That's right." She might be tired, but not so much so that she couldn't glare at me. "You think you're going to help my sister," she said skeptically. Her hand went to her mouth as she talked.

I returned the glare. "As I told Edith, I'm the best shot you have."

"And you think it's the Pattersons or Lester doing this."

I nodded. "Or the man who got her pregnant."

"It wasn't them."

"Do you have any other ideas?"

She stared at me long and hard, then gave me a slight shrug. "Edith said you wanted to talk to me, so talk."

"Tell me about the Pattersons."

"If you think they're involved, you're crazy." I waited. She finally continued. "They had a small farm outside of Burlington, but they were barely able to make it profitable. God bless Ralph, but he just isn't much of a farmer. I was friends with Gladys's sister, who lived in Limon, and I taught her kids. That's how I found out about Gladys and Ralph and how they wanted kids, but couldn't have any. The sister used to talk about how hard it was on Gladys. So when Edith got herself into trouble and didn't want to tell Gordon, I thought about the Pattersons."

"What made you think you could trust them?"

"In here." She jabbed her stomach. "My gut told me they were all right. They're good people, and they wouldn't want to do anything that would mess this up for them, or for the boy. They gave up the farm in Burlington, and I helped them find the place outside of Vernon. It was far enough away so folks wouldn't know that they had the baby right away, but close enough to Gladys's sister."

"Did you pay the Pattersons to take the baby?"

She looked away, a finger tapping her lips.

"How much did you pay them?" I asked.

"Two hundred dollars," she finally whispered. "It was all I had in savings. It was only to help them out."

"Did they think you would help them in the future?"

"They asked for money one more time, but I didn't have any to give them." She sniffled. "It wasn't about the money for them."

We'd see about that, I thought. "What about Gladys's sister? She knew that Gladys couldn't have kids."

"She swore to Gladys and me that she would keep it quiet. She never even told her husband."

"And you believe her?"

She nodded emphatically. "Yes, I do."

I wished I felt the same way. There were too many people who knew about Edith and the baby.

"Where's the sister now?"

"She's here in Denver. Her husband died – a bad heart – so she moved here and got a job during the war. She's living with a friend."

"What's her name?"

"I can't tell you that."

I suddenly leaned forward. "You better, if you want me to get to the bottom of this." She sat back, startled. "Any of these people could be blackmailing Edith, or they could've told someone else. And now we have someone who wants a lot of money from her."

"Edith doesn't have any money."

I pointed a finger at her. "But you do." She looked at me funny. "Your father had a coin collection, right?" I went on. "Who has it now?"

"I do. My father wanted me to have it, I suppose because I helped out so much. I've just held onto it for now. I figured if Edith or I ever got into money trouble, we could sell it."

"It sounds like she needs it now," I said dryly.

Her lips formed a hard line. "That's the problem. We can't keep paying whoever this is."

I held up my hands. "And yet you don't seem to want me to help you."

"You can't bother the Pattersons," she insisted. "It would scare them to death, and they were good to us, taking the boy for us."

"Have you seen Gerry?"

"I was out there a time or two, when he was still a baby. But we decided it was best if I didn't visit anymore, or someone might get suspicious. But I promised them we would leave them alone until Gerry grew up, and if he wanted to know about his mama then, we'd talk about it. So you can't tell them you know."

"I need the sister's name," I said.

She didn't answer. I waited. She waited. The silence stretched between us like a chasm. A car passed on the street, its headlights momentarily flashing past the window. I'd been to war. I'd waited long hours, motionless and quiet, to evade an enemy. I could deal with silence. She couldn't.

"Fine. It's Thelma Blanchard," she finally said. "She used to live in north Denver. But you can't let her think Edith and I are going to bother her or her sister."

I put my hands on my knees. "I'll do what I can, but we've got a real problem here. Now it's not just the Pattersons, but Gladys's sister, Thelma, and your husband, Lester."

"Ex-husband," she said harshly.

"Tell me about him."

"What's to tell? He wasn't a good man. He was looking for someone to take care of him, and I was dumb enough to do it." She stared off into space. "He wasn't a hard worker, and every time we got a little money, he'd spend it drinking or gambling."

"Why'd you marry him?"

She wagged her head in disgust. "I ask myself that." She took a long minute to form her words. "I was tired, I think. I'd spent my teen years raising Edith, and then I had to help my father when his heart started to fail. I think I was looking for a way out." She put her hands in her lap. "But I'm doing okay now."

"What did Lester say when Edith came to live with you?"

"He wasn't around, so there wasn't anything to tell him."

"But he found out about her, right?"

"Unfortunately. He showed up one day and we got into a fight. I tried to keep him out of the house. The fool thought I had a man around, and he stormed into the house and found Edith in the bedroom. She was eight months along, and there wasn't any way she could hide her pregnancy. Didn't Edith tell you this?"

"No," I said.

"Lester hooted and hollered about her getting herself into trouble. I gave him what for and kicked him out the door."

"But he shows up periodically, looking for money."

"That's right. The last time was about a month ago."

"He could be blackmailing Edith."

She let out a harsh laugh. "If he wants money, he comes to me for it."

I shook my head. "He knows by this point that you'll fight with him. Maybe he's realized he won't get any from you, so he's going after Edith. He knows she wasn't able to take care of herself, and that she goes to you when she's in trouble."

Her face fell. "I hadn't thought of that."

"Did he know about the coin collection?"

"I don't know. I never told him about it, but my father might have."

"So he may know you have access to a potential money source."

She started rocking back and forth. "Lester, if I get my hands on you."

"What does he look like?"

She pushed herself out of the chair and went to the back of the house. I heard her rummaging around and she returned with a photo in an old wooden frame.

"I don't know why I keep this," she said as she handed it to me.

It was a wedding photo of the two of them. Lester wore a black suit with cowboy boots. He was tall and rather gaunt, with thinning brown hair and hollow cheeks. He had a wild look in his eyes and a smirk on his face as he held Ruby by her elbow. She wore a simple white dress with lace and a tiny veil. Her expression seemed timid and slightly apprehensive, as if she already knew what she was getting herself into.

I gave it back to her. "Do you have any idea where Lester is now?"

"A bar somewhere." She laughed bitterly at her own joke.

"Do you think he's here in town?"

"Most likely. I got a letter from him about a month ago.

Hold on." She went to the other room again and returned with an envelope. She took a piece of paper from it and handed it to me. It was written in a scrawl I could barely read. Lester asked Ruby to please let him come home, that he'd gotten a steady job and wasn't drinking as much. It was signed simply, with just his name. No "I love you," or anything else heartfelt. I pointed to the envelope.

"Is there a return address?"

She turned it over. "Yes." She showed it to me.

"That's off Twentieth and Larimer. Downtown," I observed. "Not a very good neighborhood."

"Probably all he could afford," she said, derision in her voice.

I read the letter again. "Any idea where he was working?"

"I don't know. All he ever did was odd jobs, and it wouldn't surprise me if he was lying."

I handed the letter back to her. "Did you respond?"

"No."

"And that's the last you've heard from him?"

"Yes." She stared down at me. "If he comes around again, I'll wring his neck."

I wouldn't put it past her to do just that.

"What do you know about Fred Cooper?" I asked, turning the conversation to Edith's old flame.

"Who?"

"The man Edith was with."

She wrinkled up her lips. "I never even knew his name, and I didn't meet him, either. I don't know anything about him because Edith wouldn't tell me." I started to tell her about what Edith had said, but she waved a hand to stop me. "I don't want to know. As far as I'm concerned, he didn't live up to his obligations. He took advantage of a lonely, naïve girl and I can't forgive him for that. He's another one that if I got my hands on..." She didn't finish.

93

"Have you heard of Sonny O'Hara?"

"Who's that?"

"He's the man who met Edith in the park and took the money from her." I described him.

"He doesn't sound like anyone I know."

"Keep your eye out for him, and if you see him, you call me." I took out a card and handed it to her.

She took it and then stared at the floor. We stayed like that for a while.

"What are you telling Gordon?" she finally asked.

"Nothing about this," I said. "I'd just as soon Edith tell him about her affair. For now, I'm putting him off until I can figure out what's going on."

A pounding on the front door startled us.

"Come on, Ruby, let me in!" a deep male voice hollered. "I'm in trouble!"

"Oh my gosh!" Ruby leaped up.

I glanced at the door. "Lester?"

"Yes. I don't believe this!" Accusation flared in her eyes. "Did he follow you?"

"Not that I know of."

She ran to the door and flung it open. "Lester, get out of here!"

I went and stood behind her. Lester stood on the porch, squinting at us. He looked much older than the picture Ruby had just shown me. His hair was a bit longer and he was a lot thinner. He wobbled on his feet as he glowered at Ruby. Then he saw me.

"Who's he?" Lester said. A cloud of alcohol breath floated toward Ruby and me.

"He's a detective," Ruby snapped. She raised a hand at him. "Now go on, git!"

Lester glared at us, then whirled around. He stumbled, righted himself, and started toward the street.

"Lester," I called after him. He flung a hand at me and kept going.

"I'll be right back," I said to Ruby. Then I bolted out the door.

CHAPTER FOURTEEN

"Hey!" I yelled at Lester.

He had made it to the street and was staggering toward First Street. He mumbled something and kept going.

"Lester! I want to talk to you," I said.

"Who are you?" he slurred. He only had on a thin coat, and he hunched his shoulders against the cold.

"Dewey Webb." I trotted to catch up with him.

He squinted at me. "I got nothin' to say to you."

I grabbed his arm and he shook me off. "What kind of trouble are you in?" He kept walking and I fell in step with him. "You need money and you want to tap Ruby for some?"

"She's my wife."

"Ex-wife, and she doesn't want to give you another dime."

"Figures," he said. "I'm in a jam and she won't help."

"What kind of a jam?" I asked.

"Take a powder," he snarled. "I'm not talking to you."

"Are you bugging Edith, too?"

"That tramp," he spat out. "She deserves what she gets."

"Do you know Sonny O'Hara?"

"Beat it."

He clamped his jaw shut and quickened his pace. We reached Galapago Street. A bus was slowing down near the corner and Lester made an awkward run to it.

"Are you living on Twentieth Street?"

"That ain't none of your business."

He flagged the bus and it stopped. The door opened and he stepped through the doorway without another word to me. The door closed and he was gone.

I hoofed it back to Ruby's house. She must've been peeking out the window because the door opened before I knocked.

"What happened?" she asked.

I ignored that. "Why'd you tell him about me? If he's black-mailing Edith, now he knows someone is after him."

She turned red. "I wasn't thinking."

"Well, there's nothing we can do about it now."

I pointed past her, to my hat still sitting on the loveseat.

"Oh," she said as she looked back into the room. She scurried over to the loveseat and retrieved my hat. "What'd he tell you?"

"Nothing." I put on my hat. "He's too soused to know his head from his tail."

"Typical," she said.

"What kind of trouble is he in?"

She shrugged. "How should I know? It's better he's gone."

I studied her. "You haven't seen him in a month?"

"That's right. You saw what he's like. Why would I want to deal with that anymore?"

"Okay. I'll talk to him when he's sobered up and see if he knows anything." I turned to go.

"Thank you," she said.

I nodded. I must've gained her trust. The door clicked shut as I walked to my car. I'd told Ruby I wanted to wait until Lester had sobered up, but in truth, I wanted to talk to him again while he was drunk. With a little more pushing, maybe his lips would loosen and he'd say something he wouldn't when he sobered up. So instead of going home, I drove north on Santa Fe. If Lester went straight home, I'd beat him there driving while he was on the bus. Provided the address on Twentieth was his. Regardless, I could ask around and see if anyone knew him.

Fifteen minutes later, I turned onto Twentieth and found the address that was on the envelope Lester had sent to Ruby. It was a four-story brick building with narrow windows and fire escapes zigzagging up either side. An arc of light lit the doorway, but the small lawn in front of the building was in shadows. I parked and killed the headlights, and the street was plunged into darkness. No one was around. This was not the kind of neighborhood to be wandering around at night.

I felt for my gun, then got out and started up the walk. As I neared the door, I heard a voice coming from the side of the building. A guy in a long coat appeared. He saw me and stopped.

"You got any money?" he asked.

I shook my head. "Does Lester Klassen live here?"

"How the hell do I know?" he said, then crossed the lawn and sauntered down the street. Soon the blackness swallowed him.

I went inside the building and checked a panel of mailboxes, but they weren't labeled. Apartment 302 had been on the address on the envelope, so I climbed the stairs to the third floor. An overhead light dimly lit a long hallway. I walked quietly down a wood floor to 302 and stopped and listened at the door. Nothing. I knocked and waited. No one answered. I put my ear to the door and listened, but didn't hear anything. I tried the knob. Locked. I walked over to 301 and was about to knock when loud voices came from the other side. A man was yelling, and then a dame hollered back at him. I lowered my hand. I wasn't going to interrupt whatever dispute was in progress. I tramped back to the stairs, hurried down, and went outside.

I stood for a moment in the cold and looked around. The door to a bar on the corner opened and blues music blasted into the street. The bar was so nondescript it didn't even have a name, just a sign over the door that read "Bar." Two men came out and the door slammed shut behind them. The music died and they started toward me. I eyed them warily, but they passed by me and toward the apartment door.

"Does Lester Klassen live around here?" I called after them.

"Yeah, third floor," one of them said.

His buddy eyed me. "Man, what's Lester up to?" He was heavy with thinning red hair, and he slurred his words.

"Huh?" I said.

The first guy studied me as well. "Yeah, all these snobby visitors."

"Who's been visiting him?" I asked.

"Aw, lay off," the redhead growled.

They ambled inside the building without another word.

What snobby visitors had been to see Lester? I puzzled over that as I went to the Plymouth. It was now close to seven and I was tired and hungry, so I drove home.

———

Clara was sitting in the living room, holding a wailing Sam, when I came in.

"Hi," she said in a harried voice. Her hair was disheveled and she had dark circles under her eyes. It had obviously been a long day for her. She stood up. "Can you take him, please? I need a break."

I leaned down and kissed her, then picked up Sam. "Hey, buddy," I cooed at him.

She nodded toward the kitchen. "I'll fix you something to eat in a minute."

"Take your time." I held Sam close to my chest and began pacing the room.

"Someone named Gordon Sandalwood called a couple of times. He wants you to call him back."

"Okay, thanks."

Clara went into the kitchen while I continued to pace, and I quietly sang him "Little Boy Blue," an old lullaby my mother had sung to me when I was little. Sam cried for a bit more, but then he quieted down. I put Sam down in his crib, then went into the bedroom and slipped off my coat, then put my gun in a box in the closet.

I checked on Sam once more, assured myself that he was asleep, and then went into the kitchen. Clara was at the sink.

"He's been fussy all day," she said as she brushed a strand of hair out of her eye.

I strolled over and kissed her on the cheek. "You're doing a great job."

She threw me a tired smile. "Thanks." Then she nodded toward the phone. "You'd better call that fellow back."

"Okay." I fixed a Scotch and soda, then sipped it while I dialed Sandalwood's number. If Edith answered, I hoped she wouldn't recognize my voice, since we weren't supposed to know about each other. Luckily, Sandalwood picked up the phone.

"It's Dewey." I kicked out a chair and sat down at the kitchen table.

"What's going on? Have you found out anything?"

"Not yet. I'm following some leads," I said cagily. "What's going on with Edith?"

"She's a wreck. She's nervous about something, but she won't tell me anything. What's got her so worked up?"

"Give me a little more time, and we'll get to the bottom of this."

"I hope so." His voice was laced with worry. "I don't know what to do anymore. Maybe she needs to see someone – a psychoanalyst."

"Give me a few more days before you make a decision." Even though I'd first suggested a psychoanalyst, now I was steering him away from that idea...but I had more information than I'd had before.

He grudgingly agreed, and I told him I'd update him again soon, and then hung up. I sipped my Scotch and wondered about Edith. By the time I found out who was blackmailing her, she might indeed need some analysis because the stress would drive her to it. I still wished she would tell her husband what was happening, but I wasn't going to push her on that. For now, I'd see what I could find out about the suspects I had.

I set my glass down, pulled a phone directory from a kitchen drawer, and thumbed through the 'C's. And listed there were two Frederick Coopers. One address was on the east side of town, near Lowry Air Force Base, so I figured I'd try that one first. That made me wonder if Cooper was still in the military. I'd see if I could find him tomorrow, but I wanted to have as much information on him as I could before I spoke to him. That way, if he lied to me about anything, I'd catch him. But how to get the dirt on him?

"I forgot to ask, how was your day?" Clara interrupted my thoughts.

"It was okay," I said. I jotted down Fred Cooper's address in a notepad I carried, then put the phone directory aside.

Clara pulled the meatloaf from the oven and then used the MixMaster to whip up a bowl of potatoes. I sipped my drink and watched her. Even after the baby, her dark brown dress complimented her figure nicely. I kept my hands to myself, though. She was pretty enticing, but I was awfully hungry. The kitchen was warm, and I took a minute to forget everything but her.

"Do you think you could get one of the neighbors to watch Sam, and we'll go to the Rainbow Ballroom?" I asked. "And we can dance like we used to?" The Rainbow Ballroom was a popular dance hall, and the largest indoor hall in Colorado.

She set a bottle of milk on the table and smiled at me. "That would be lovely."

We hadn't been out in a long time. Between having a baby and my quitting the law office where I'd been an investigator to go out on my own, there hadn't been time or money. Worry crossed her face.

"Is the job getting to you?"

I shook my head. "It's okay."

But I couldn't fool her. I had been concerned lately about getting enough work. Right now we were squeaking by. I didn't want to go back to the law office with my tail between my legs and beg for a job. I wanted to make my own business successful, but I also had to make sure I could provide for Clara and Sam.

Clara put filled plates and silverware on the table, and we ate and chatted. Afterward, she did the dishes while we talked more, and then I read the paper while she knitted and listened to one of her favorite radio programs, *Casey, Crime Photographer*. But I kept thinking about her and my job. She wanted to be by my side, whatever I did, but I know the lack of a steady paycheck troubled her. I think she secretly wished I would tire of private work and go back to the law office. Someday I might have to, but I wasn't ready to do that just yet. I still had a case to solve.

CHAPTER FIFTEEN

Shortly before eight the next morning, I drove down Larimer Street to Twentieth, to Lester's apartment. The street didn't seem quite so ominous in the daylight, but that didn't mean the neighborhood was any safer. It was Friday, a workday, and not as many cars were parked on the street as last night, presumably because most people were at work. I found a place right in front of his building and pulled the Plymouth into it, got out, and strolled up to the entrance. No one was about, and the bar next door was silent. When I went inside, it was quiet as well.

I took the stairs two at a time to the third floor and was greeted with an eerie stillness. I found Lester's unit and knocked on the door. I waited, then banged harder, rattling the old wood door. The sound reverberated up and down the empty hall. I raised my fist and was about to knock again when a door across the hall opened. I turned around. One of the men I'd seen last night poked his head out.

"What's all the racket, man?" His red hair stuck out in tufts all over his head, his eyes were bloodshot, and he was a little pale.

"Have you seen Lester?" I asked.

"Na. He's probably sleeping it off." He blinked at me wearily. "Come back later, okay?" He slammed his door shut.

I waited a minute, then tried Lester's doorknob. Locked. I rapped on the door one more time, not caring what the neighbor thought, but still no answer. I kicked the door, frustrated that I wasn't able to rouse Lester now, and that I'd have to come back later to talk to him. I tramped downstairs and back to the Plymouth. I lit a cigarette and watched his building while I smoked. A few minutes later, a woman in a threadbare overcoat and shabby shoes walked out the door. She pulled a scarf down over her head and started for the corner. A bit after that, the man across the hall from Lester emerged. He didn't look any better now. He weaved his way around the side of the building and was gone. But no Lester. I finally started up the Plymouth and left.

I drove to a gas station and found a pay phone with a phone directory. I checked the book, hoping to find Sonny O'Hara listed. I wanted to call him and see if he was home. I still wasn't ready to talk to him yet, but if I could follow him for a while, he might lead me to whoever was blackmailing Edith. Unfortunately, he wasn't listed. Probably couldn't afford a phone. That meant I'd need to try to see if he was home without his knowing it.

When I arrived in Sonny's neighborhood, I parked around the corner and walked back toward his apartment building. I stopped and leaned against a leafless maple tree near a bus stop and pretended to wait for the next one. While I did so, I looked up to Sonny's apartment window. The curtains weren't drawn, but I didn't see any movement inside. I waited for a while, and then I finally strolled across the lawn and into the building.

The same rank odor hit me again, this time stronger. I

wondered if a rodent had died somewhere nearby and no one had discovered its rotting body. I ignored the smell as I tiptoed up the stairs, hoping I was quiet enough not to alert the landlady to my presence. The last thing I wanted was for her to appear and make a fuss that Sonny could hear, if he was home. I was halfway up the stairs when the door at the bottom of the stairs opened.

"Who's there?" a familiar voice warbled, too loudly for my taste.

I whirled around.

"Oh, it's you." The landlady came into the hallway with a flourish. Today she was in a light blue flowered dress instead of her pink housecoat, but it didn't fit any better. She had curled her thinning gray hair and had put on bright red lipstick. "I thought you were my friend. We're going out to brunch."

"That's nice," I said as I trotted back down the stairs.

She looked past me. "If you're looking for Sonny, he's not there."

"He already left this morning?"

"Yes, along with that other fellow."

"The one with the slicked-back hair," I said.

"That's the one. He stood out front and smoked for a while until Sonny finally showed up."

"Sonny wasn't upstairs?"

She shook her head. "He didn't come home last night, at least not that I heard." She may not have heard him, but if she was awake, I had no doubt she would've seen him. She seemed to keep tabs on everyone. Her lips went in and out, smearing her lipstick. "And they made quite a ruckus this morning, too."

"What happened?"

"They were arguing." She leaned against the doorjamb. "Mind you, I don't meddle in other people's business."

"Of course not," I said. And yet she had so much to share with me. "What were they arguing about?"

"I just happened to look out the door for my friend, and Sonny and this fellow were going upstairs. But then they stopped and Sonny said he didn't want to keep going back to her, that they should just get it all at one time."

"All of what?"

She shrugged. "I'm just repeating what I heard. I wasn't going to ask because I don't meddle."

"Right. Go on."

"And the other fellow said 'We'll do what he says, got it?' And then he said, 'You'll get your cut either way, so shut your trap, you hear me?' Sonny wasn't happy about hearing that."

"You saw him?"

"I didn't have to. I could hear it in his voice, and he cursed, too."

"Did they talk about anything else?"

"Sonny said something about he's the one having to meet her, not everyone else. And the other fellow told him to shut up." She stared at me, her incessant lip-twitching driving me to distraction.

"That's all?"

"Yes. They were upstairs for a few minutes, and then they came back down and left. I made sure they didn't see me. Sonny was so angry."

Just then, the outside door opened and another gray-haired woman walked in.

"Oh," she said when she saw us standing there. "Why, hello, Catherine."

"Is it time to go already?" Catherine said. She grabbed a gray wool overcoat from inside her apartment and slipped into it. It was a few sizes too big and almost touched the floor. Then she glanced at me. "If you talk to Sonny, you tell him he better not bring any trouble around here because I've got enough as it is."

"Is there a problem?" the woman said as she eyed me suspiciously.

"No, dear." Catherine shuffled over to her and patted her arm. "Let's go."

With that, they left. I stood in the doorway and watched them walk slowly to an old Ford. Her friend helped Catherine get in, and then as she walked around to the driver's side, she gave me a stern look. I felt like telling her I wasn't like the characters who lived here, but she was already getting into the car. The Ford grumbled to life and eased down the street.

I waited until they disappeared, then stepped outside and shut the door behind me. I breathed in the fresh air and wondered about Sonny and his pal. It sounded like they were getting ready to ask Edith for more money. A lot more. But how did they know she had money to surrender? Did they know about her father's coin collection? They must've thought she had it, or had access to it. Sonny and his pal apparently were taking orders from someone else. I frowned. Edith was in big trouble unless I could find out who was giving those orders.

My eyes roved around and I saw a few cigarette butts lying in the dirt next to the door. I bent down and picked up one. It had been hand-rolled. I sniffed it, but didn't recognize any particular odor. There had been tobacco and rolling paper at the Pattersons' house. Ralph's? Had he been here? It was a stretch, but one never knew. I tossed the butt aside, stood up and strolled back to my car. I needed more information on Sonny and the others, and I knew where to find it. I'd go by the law office, but I wouldn't be asking for a job, as Clara might have hoped, but for information.

CHAPTER SIXTEEN

I showed up at Masters and O'Reilly shortly after ten. The law offices were located on the eighth floor of the Continental Oil Building, at Eighteenth and Glenarm Place. The building was an impressive ten stories, made of polished granite and terra-cotta facing, with a huge, red electric Conoco sign on top of the building. At night, the sign lit up and you could see it for miles. When I walked into the office, the receptionist narrowed her eyes.

"Hello, Miriam," I said, and made a show of tipping my hat. She wore a strong perfume that always made me wrinkle my nose. Which never helped her disposition.

"Dewey," she said coolly.

Miriam Malloy looked like a movie star, with perfect, curly brown hair, sultry eyes, and soft skin, but underneath she was a hard woman. We'd never been fond of each other, and it hadn't changed since I'd left to go out on my own.

"Is Chet in?" I asked.

"Yes, but..." she started to say, but then I noticed a man in a gray suit coming down the hallway toward the front desk. He saw me and a huge smile spread across his face.

"Dewey, old boy," he said. He held out his hand and I shook it.

Chet Inglewood was about ten years older than I was, with brown hair that was graying at the temples, and dark eyes that missed nothing. I'd met him when I first started working at Masters and O'Reilly, right after I returned from the war. He was about my height, but a bit heavier, all of it muscle. He had an easygoing demeanor, and that, along with a soft tenor voice, made people underestimate him. And those who did regretted it.

He pointed at the door with his brown fedora. "I'm late for an appointment. Can you walk with me?"

"That'll work," I said.

He glanced at Miriam. "I'll be back later this afternoon." He smoothed his dark hair and put on his hat.

"That'll be fine," she said, as if she had any say.

Chet had been the chief investigator at Masters and O'Reilly for a number of years, except for the time he served during the war, and he came and went as he wanted. He certainly didn't need to ask for permission from Miriam to leave. He was a top-notch investigator who didn't take any guff from anyone, and I'd learned a lot from him.

"Do you want your overcoat?" she asked him.

"No, it's warm today."

He glanced at me as we stepped into the hallway and strolled to the elevators. "That woman won't help with something I need if I beg her, but she'll mother me to death."

I laughed. That sounded like the Miriam I remembered.

He pushed the elevator button. "What's going on?"

"I'm hoping you can provide me a little information," I said.

He cocked an eyebrow. "A new case?"

I nodded.

"How are things?"

I hemmed and hawed. "Not bad. It could be busier."

"I'll keep sending you what I can."

When he could, Chet threw business my way, and I was grateful for that. He was also willing to help out whenever he could, and since he was in contact with a lot of people, he was a wealth of information. If he didn't know someone, it was a good bet he knew of them and about them.

"I thought this one was going to be easy," I continued, "but it's not turning out that way."

"I'm headed down to the police station to talk to a contact there," he said as the elevator arrived. "But I can give you a few minutes." We rode in silence to the lobby and out to the street. It was warmer than it had been in days, pleasant for a walk. "I'm parked down the street," he said.

As we headed down Glenarm, I began. "I'm looking for information on a guy named Fred Cooper. He used to be an officer in the Army Air Force. He was out at Lowry."

"I was a Navy man."

"I remember that. I was in the army."

"Right, so that's no help," he said with a wry laugh. We stopped at the corner and waited to cross the street. "I've got a buddy who works out at Lowry. Let me see if I can get ahold of him and see if he knows this guy. Fred Cooper, you say?"

I nodded.

"Why are you looking into him?"

"He had an affair with my client's wife."

He glanced at me, so I briefly told him about Edith being blackmailed and my list of suspects. The light changed and we continued down the next block.

"What makes you think Cooper would do that to Edith?" he asked.

"I don't know, but he's one of a handful of people who knew about the pregnancy – obviously – or he could've told someone else about it."

"This way," he said, and we cut through a parking lot to a Plymouth sedan that was much nicer than mine. The sun was out and he shielded his eyes as he looked at me. "If someone had loose lips and talked about Edith's pregnancy, your suspect list could be huge."

I sighed. "I know. It has to be someone who wants money and knows that Edith has the money to give them. I'm looking into those that knew about the pregnancy first."

"And see what you can shake out of the tree," he said.

"Right."

"And so you're going to talk to Cooper, who fathered the baby?"

I rubbed my chin. "I tried to talk to Lester Klassen last night –"

"The sister's ex, right?" he interjected.

"Yeah. Have you heard of him?"

He shook his head. "But I'll keep my ears open."

"He was tight, and belligerent, so my brief conversation with him was pointless. I stopped by his place this morning, when he might be sober, to see what he knows, but he was either still sleeping it off or he wasn't there. He said last night that he's in some kind of trouble. If I can find him and press him a bit, he might spill what's going on. It may not have anything to do with Edith, but I've got to start eliminating suspects."

"And you've got Gladys Patterson's sister to talk to, right? She knew about Edith. That might lead somewhere." Chet didn't miss a thing.

"That's right." I scrutinized him closely. "Are you trying to steer me away from Fred Cooper?"

He hesitated. "Maybe. You need to be careful. If he's even still with the Air Force, he could be a pretty high rank by now. And if you make trouble for him, it could come back on you. You don't work with me anymore, so there's no way I can cover for you."

"I know. I'll be careful."

He unlocked the car door, slid behind the wheel and rolled down the window. "I'll be back in the office by six. Call me, and I'll let you know what I find out."

"That'll be great." I held up a hand. "One more thing. Have you heard of Sonny O'Hara?"

He frowned. "He's involved in this?"

"He's the one who took the money from Edith, but he told her he was just the middleman. I need to find out how he's connected to this, too."

"Sonny's a small-time hood. He grew up around here, and he's been in and out of jail for years. But I've never heard of him blackmailing anyone. That doesn't seem like his style."

"That's why I didn't talk to him right away. If I spook him, he'll warn off the bigger fish."

"I'm sure there is one," he said. "Sonny doesn't have the gumption to do something like this on his own."

"The landlady said she saw him with a big guy with dark, slicked-back hair. She said he was kind of greasy." I shrugged. "It's not much of a description."

"I don't know who Sonny's hanging around these days. And I don't see him doing this type of thing, but I guess anything's possible."

"Sonny's landlady overheard him and another guy talking about asking Edith for more money all at once. I don't think they're going to stop until they've bled her dry."

Chet shook his head. "I wonder what Sonny's gotten involved in."

"If you hear anything about him or the dark-haired guy, let me know."

"Sure thing. And be careful with Sonny. He likes to carry a blade with him, and he knows how to use it. I saw a guy he knifed, and it wasn't pretty."

"Thanks for the warning."

"I've got to get going." He started the car. "How are Clara and Sam?"

"They're great," I said.

"Tell Clara I said hello."

"I will."

I thanked him and watched as he drove out of the parking lot. I had more information now, but it hadn't helped to clear up much.

CHAPTER SEVENTEEN

Ten minutes later, I arrived at my office. I let myself in, grabbed the mail that had been shoved through a slot in the door, and took a few minutes to check it. I put some bills on the desk and threw out the rest, and then I grabbed a manila folder from a drawer and started a file on Gordon and Edith Sandalwood. I prepared a list of expenses incurred so far and put receipts with them. I put it all into the folder, and then I jotted down a few notes in a journal that I kept. Once I finished, I filed the folder in a cabinet and put the journal back in my desk drawer under some blank paper where it couldn't be seen.

I pulled out a telephone directory and looked up Thelma Blanchard. She was still listed with an address in north Denver. It was time to pay her a visit to see what she might know. I thought about the cigarette butts I'd found outside Sonny's apartment building. It was a long shot, but if Ralph was in town to see Sonny, maybe he had paid his sister-in-law a visit, too. I wrote down her address and phone number in the notepad, along with Fred Cooper's address, then locked up and left.

Breakfast had been a long time ago, so I stopped at a Rockybilt on Colfax for a quick bite. I ordered several of the greasy burger with the special sauce that I loved, and while I ate, I puzzled over Sonny O'Hara. How had he gotten involved in blackmailing Edith? What was his connection to whoever was masterminding this little scheme? I didn't know yet, but I hoped that by the time I'd visited with Thelma Blanchard and Fred Cooper, the connection between them might become clearer.

———

The street Thelma lived on meandered down a hill and curved to the north. It was a quaint neighborhood off 50th Avenue, northwest of downtown, with a mix of houses that had been built at the turn of the century and newer homes, so the styles varied. I walked up the steps of a small ranch and knocked on the door. The woman who answered was big-boned and a little heavy, with blond hair twisted into a bun so tight that it seemed to pull the skin back on her face. A small white cat slithered around her legs, then gazed up at me with lazy eyes and meowed.

"Yes?" she said in a high, squeaky voice that didn't seem to fit her large bearing.

"Are you Thelma Blanchard?" I asked.

"Yes." She reached down, picked up the cat and cooed at it.

"My name is Dewey Webb and I'm a private detective."

A sharp intake of breath. "What do you want?"

I moved in hard and fast. "I'd like to ask you a few questions about Edith Sandalwood."

"Who?"

"Edith Sandalwood," I repeated. "She's the sister of Ruby Klassen."

The stern look on her face remained, but I noticed the

slightest flicker in her eyes. "I'm sorry, I don't know either of those women."

"That's how you want to play it?" I said harshly.

"I...I'm sure I don't know what you mean." She started to shut the door.

"Edith Sandalwood had a baby and she gave it to your sister Gladys," I said hurriedly. The door stopped. "Look, lady, I'm in no mood for games."

She blinked hard a few times, and then opened the door wider and stepped aside. "I guess you better come in." She led me into a small living area with a long sofa and a blond-wood coffee table. She sat at one end of the sofa and pointed for me to sit at the other. She crossed her arms and contemplated me, still trying for defiant. The cat sat next to her and scowled at me as well. "Ruby promised that she wouldn't tell anyone about us."

"She didn't want me to talk to you, but you could be involved in this."

"In what?" she asked as she nervously stroked the cat. "What do you know about Gladys?"

If she knew anything at all about the blackmailing, she was playing it well. She appeared genuinely surprised by my presence and my questions.

"I've been out to Vernon and I've talked to your sister," I said. "And I've seen Gerry."

She caught her breath in a little choking sound. "You saw Gerry?"

I nodded. "He's the spitting image of Edith."

She recovered herself and glared at me. "I don't understand. Gladys would've never said anything about Gerry. She's too scared that someone might report them."

"Report them for what?"

"It wasn't an official adoption. What if the authorities found out and decided to take Gerry away from them?"

"I doubt that would happen."

"Maybe, but we weren't going to take any chances, so we never told anyone about Edith's pregnancy, or that Gladys had taken Gerry."

"No one?"

"Yes," she said, slightly indignant. "You don't believe me?"

I shrugged. "I don't know who to believe."

"What's going on?" she asked. "Why are you here?"

"*Someone* knows that Edith had an affair while her husband was away and that she got pregnant. And someone is threatening to tell Edith's husband unless she pays up big."

She gasped. "That's terrible!"

The cat jumped at the sound of her voice. He stretched and then came over to me.

"Whoever it is wants a lot of money," I said. The cat rubbed up against my legs.

"It's not me. And it's not Gladys or Ralph, either. Ruby didn't tell us why Edith was giving up the baby, and we never asked."

I frowned. "How can you be so sure Gladys or Ralph aren't behind this? From what I saw, they took money from Ruby once, and they're hurting for dough."

"They did take money, but only because they needed the help." She looked at me with pleading eyes. "He's their boy now. They may be poor, but they're proud, and they'd never resort to blackmail." She choked up. "And I told you, they wouldn't do anything that could mean they might lose Gerry."

"What about you?"

The cat suddenly jumped into my lap. I petted it, and it purred.

She put a hand to her chest. "Me? Why would I do anything to Edith?"

"You're a widow." I gestured at the meager surroundings. "I'll bet money's tight."

She narrowed her eyes at me. "That may be true, but I've never done a crooked thing in my life. And although I've sometimes questioned my sister's decision, that boy has been a blessing for them, and I'd never do anything that might cause them to lose him."

"You didn't think they should take Gerry in?"

"They've never had any money, and he was one more mouth to feed." She let out a long sigh. "But...they wanted a baby so badly. And they've never been happier."

"Tell me about Sonny O'Hara," I said, hoping to catch her off-guard.

"Who?" The name meant nothing to her.

"He's got brown hair and likes to wear a pork pie hat."

"I don't know him."

There was something in her countenance that made me believe that she was telling the truth. She was sure in her answers, but not so much so that she appeared calculating. If she was covering up something, she might volunteer some bits of information to me, but hold back on others. Instead, she seemed straightforward with everything. But that didn't mean the Pattersons were in the clear. They could be blackmailing Edith without Thelma having any idea.

"Did you know Lester?" I asked. "Ruby's husband?"

She gave me a look of disdain as she got up, came over and gestured for the cat. "That good-for-nothing bum. Is he still bothering Ruby?"

I nodded as I handed it to her. "I saw him last night."

"That figures." She stroked the cat in a calming manner.

"He'll take every cent Ruby has, if she lets him. I think he stole money from her father, too, when he was still alive."

"How do you know that?"

"Ruby mentioned it, a long time ago. From what I understand, her father was awfully upset at Lester, and at Ruby for marrying him."

I'd have to check with Ruby about that. "And Lester knew about Edith's pregnancy?" I asked Thelma.

"I don't know. He wasn't around much, and Edith was trying to stay out of sight, so no one would know about her." She suddenly stifled a sob and clutched the cat to her. He meowed loudly. "Mr. Webb, I'm very sorry about what's happening to Edith, but I don't know anything. You've got to believe me."

If it was an act, it was good. "Has Ralph been to see you lately?"

"No." She sniffled. "They rarely come into Denver. That old truck he has isn't very reliable, and they can't afford the gas."

I stood up. "If I find out you're lying to me –"

"I'm not," she said testily. She collected herself and showed me to the door. "Please don't tell anyone about the...situation with Gerry. It's better that way."

"As long as you're not blackmailing Edith, I have no reason to."

"Of course I'm not," she repeated.

I went outside and she quietly shut the door behind me. As I strolled to the Plymouth, I saw that she'd moved to the front window where she could watch me. She was still petting the cat. I was sure the first thing she'd do would be to call Gladys and tell her about my visit. I was okay with that. If Gladys and Ralph were blackmailing Edith and they found out a private detective was looking into it, maybe they'd get scared and make a mistake. And I'd be ready for it.

CHAPTER EIGHTEEN

Since I still didn't know much about Fred Cooper, I decided I would wait to see if he came home at a reasonable time. If so, I planned to confront him and, as Chet said, see what fell out of the tree. I stopped at a pay phone and called Chet, hoping that he might've returned to the office before four. Miriam said he'd been in briefly, and had said that if I called, to tell me to call him this evening at home. I thanked her and hung up.

It was a long drive from Thelma Blanchard's to Fred Cooper's neighborhood on the east side of town. His house was one of many that were all the same, small with chimneys, tiny front porches and lawns, and single car garages. The area was close to Lowry, and a lot of military personnel lived in the neighborhood.

Fred Cooper's home was on the corner of Fourth and Quebec, one of the busier streets in the area. On the other side of the street was a Woolworth's, with a large parking lot. I pulled the Plymouth into a spot near Quebec, where I had a good view of Cooper's house. It was a little after three, and kids were walking home from school. I soon saw a small girl and a taller boy stroll up to the house. As they crossed the lawn, the front door opened and a woman in a print dress and apron waved at them. The kids started running and all three disappeared into the house. I tapped the steering wheel. If this was the correct Fred Cooper – the guy who'd gotten Edith pregnant – he still had the wife, but he'd added a couple of kids. I wondered if he ever thought of his child with Edith.

I leaned back and stretched, then glanced at my watch. If Cooper worked regular hours, I expected he would come home sometime after five. I smoked a cigarette and watched the house, but no one came out. Even though it had been a nice day, it was still too chilly for the kids to play outside. The sun sank low in the sky, the temperature began to drop, and I folded my arms to help keep warm. At half past five, a brand-new sedan came down the street, slowed and turned into the Cooper driveway. I quickly started the Plymouth, careened out of the parking lot and zipped across the street, narrowly missing a truck. It honked its horn, but I ignored it.

A tall man was just getting out of the sedan when I pulled up to the curb. He was in a blue Air Force uniform, and I saw the silver eagle on it. Cooper was still in the service, and he'd kept climbing in the military world; he was now a colonel. I rolled down my window and called out to him.

"Fred Cooper?"

He turned around and eyed me curiously. "Yes?"

"I'm Dewey Webb," I said. "I need to ask you about Edith Sandalwood."

I'd hoped the element of surprise would put him off-balance, and it worked. If he didn't know Edith, he would, in theory, be puzzled. But Cooper's eyes widened in shock and he went white as snow. Then he glanced back toward the house.

"I can't talk to you about that here," he hissed.

Thelma Blanchard had tried to lie. Cooper wasn't that

quick. But then, he had a wife and kids to think about.

"Tell me where," I said.

He was in such a panic, he could hardly speak.

"Where what?"

"Where we can talk." I threw him a wicked smile. "I'm not leaving until we do."

"Uh...meet me at the White Spot," he finally managed to say. "It's on the corner of First and Quebec."

"Fifteen minutes," I said.

"I can't get away that soon," he protested.

"Figure out a way," I gestured at the house, "or I'll come back and introduce myself to your pretty wife."

"All right," he said. He whirled around and hurried into the house.

I turned around and got back on Quebec, then drove to the White Spot. I used the restroom and then spotted a pay phone, so I called Clara to let her know that I wasn't sure when I'd be home and to eat without me.

"I'll leave something in the refrigerator for you," she said. In the background, I could hear Sam crying.

The entrance to the kitchen was nearby and waitresses came in and out of swinging doors. I turned toward the wall so they couldn't hear me. "I'm going to grab a bite soon."

"Oh, you might be *really* late."

"Yeah. Don't wait up for me." I said it, but it didn't do any good. I frequently came home well into the night and she would either be up reading or knitting, or in bed pretending to be asleep. I didn't know how to relieve her anxiety about my work, and I hoped that one day she wouldn't worry so much.

"Okay," she said, forcing cheer into her voice.

I told her I loved her and then hung up. I strolled back through the restaurant and sat in a booth in the corner. A waitress brought me coffee, and I'd barely had time to test it before

Cooper walked in. His eyes darted around the restaurant and then he saw me. He hurried over and slid in across the table. He hadn't changed clothes, but his uniform jacket was unbuttoned, his tie was askew, and he'd forgotten to wear his cap. The waitress approached again.

I cocked an eyebrow at him. "Coffee?"

Cooper shook his head, and I waved the waitress off. He ran a hand over his closely cropped blond hair, then pulled out a gold cigarette case. He withdrew a cigarette and lit it with a matching gold lighter. His hands shook the whole time.

"What's this about?" he asked.

I took a drink of my coffee and let him stay nervous. Sweat popped up on his forehead. "Edith Sandalwood," I finally said.

"Are you her husband?" He couldn't look me in the eye.

"No. He doesn't know about you."

He relaxed just a bit. He took a drag off the cigarette and blew smoke, then said, "I haven't thought of her in a long time."

"How long?" I asked.

He gazed out the window. "Since I broke up with her."

"Because she was pregnant."

He nodded. "I was – am – married. I couldn't have my wife find out."

"I suspect it could've hurt your career, too." I pointed to the eagle on his uniform.

He nodded. "Maybe." He took another drag on the cigarette. "How do you know about Edith and me?"

"She told me."

"And you are?"

"Dewey Webb. She hired me." Technically that wasn't true, but he didn't need to know that. "Someone's blackmailing her."

"Let me guess. Unless she pays up, her husband is going to find out about her and me and the pregnancy."

I nodded. "Very good."

He shook his head slowly. "I've sometimes wondered if Edith would come back to confront me, and she'd want money, but I didn't expect something like this."

"Why would you think Edith would do that?"

"I thought if she'd told her husband, he would divorce her, and then she'd need the money."

"She needs money now."

He didn't say anything to that. "Does her husband have it?"

"She hasn't told him she's being blackmailed," I pointed out.

"Right." He paused. "Then how's she going to pay the blackmailers?" I shrugged. "Huh," was all he said to that.

"Seems like it doesn't matter to you what happened to her."

He tapped ash off the cigarette. "I was looking for a little fun, that's all. Edith got serious, but it wasn't my fault. I certainly didn't love her or want a kid with her."

"I see."

"When she told me, I figured the best thing to do was break it off quick, so she wouldn't bug me anymore."

"You had a lot to lose if people found out."

He contemplated the glowing end of his cigarette. "Yes, I did."

"She did you a favor and stayed away."

"Right." He swore. "This can't come out now. I don't want to lose my family."

"You're one of a handful of people that knew about the pregnancy." I took a sip of coffee, then looked at him over the rim of the cup. "Unless you told other people about it."

"Why would I do that?"

I set the cup down. "I don't know. You were scared, so you talked to a pal. Or you bragged about your conquest."

He finished the cigarette and crushed it out in an ashtray. "I didn't tell a soul."

I waited. He pulled out another cigarette from the case and

lit it.

"How much does an officer make?" I asked.

"None of your business."

"Is money tight?"

He laughed at that. "You think I'm blackmailing her? I don't think so."

"You wouldn't tell me if you were."

He jabbed the cigarette at me. "I told you, I haven't seen Edith since I broke off the affair."

"Ever hear of Sonny O'Hara?"

"No," he said firmly.

"What about a big guy with dark, slicked-back hair?"

He shook his head. "Sounds like a lot of guys."

"What about Lester Klassen?"

"I didn't know any of Edith's family."

"I didn't say he was related to Edith."

His hand shook again. "She may have mentioned him, but I don't *know* him, so lay off."

"Did Edith talk about her family at all?"

"No." He said it too fast.

I crossed my arms and studied him. He might not know Sonny O'Hara or his dark-haired pal, but he was familiar with Edith's family. So why was he lying about it?

"I've got to get back," he suddenly announced.

"What'd you tell your wife when you left?" I asked.

"I said I forgot something at work."

"And yet you went back to the base without your cap?" I shook my head in mock disappointment.

He paled and ran a hand nervously over his head. "She won't notice."

"You better hope not," I said.

He slid from the booth and stood up. Then he pointed at me with the cigarette. "What happened with Edith was in the past. I don't know what's going on with her now, and it would be best if you leave me alone."

I threw out the card that Chet had warned me not to. "I can ask around the base, see what people will tell me about you."

His eyes narrowed. "If you do, there'll be trouble for you."

I wasn't too worried. Trouble for me would be trouble for him.

He put the cigarette in the corner of his mouth, then dug two coins from his pocket and tossed them on the table. They clinked down loudly. "The coffee's on me." He whirled around and stomped out of the restaurant.

I picked up one of the dimes he'd left and stared at it. If he thought this would keep me from bothering him again, he was wrong. He was lying, and until I found out what he was hiding, I would keep after him. I put the dime down and gulped the last of my coffee as I gazed out the window. Then I waved the waitress over and ordered more coffee and pot roast. She walked away, and I stared out into the darkness.

Fred Cooper cared only about himself. I shook my head. He hadn't asked how Edith was doing now, or anything about his child with her. What had Edith seen in him? I almost laughed at his nervousness. He could've been anxious because he didn't want the affair and pregnancy to be discovered. Or he could be worried because he was blackmailing Edith, and his scheme was unraveling. I didn't know which.

And then there was Thelma Blanchard. She didn't seem to know anything. But sometimes the one who appeared the least guilty was, in fact, the most culpable.

The waitress returned with my pot roast and I ate it quickly. Once I finished, I added a dollar bill to the dimes that Cooper had left, then slid out of the booth. I needed to talk to Chet, but in private, so I headed out to the Plymouth and drove to my office.

CHAPTER NINETEEN

Friday night traffic was busy as I drove downtown to Sherman Street. A few cars were parked up and down the block, but I was able to get a spot right in front of my office. Since it was past seven o'clock, the old Victorian was dark. I strolled up the walk and onto the porch, then tried the front door. It was supposed to be locked after hours, but sometimes that didn't happen. Tonight was one of those nights. I shook my head in disgust as I let myself in. A large foyer was lit by moonlight coming through windows on either side of the door. I locked the door behind me, crossed the foyer, and climbed the creaky stairs to the second floor.

The hallway floorboards groaned as I walked down to my office. I was about to get out my key when I noticed that the door was cracked open. I stepped back and pressed myself against the wall, then quickly drew my gun from my shoulder holster. I listened for a moment, but didn't hear anything. I peered through the crack in the door. It was completely dark inside. I raised my gun, then kicked open the door. It swung back and banged against the wall. The sound reverberated into the hall, but nothing happened. I waited a moment longer, then rushed inside, staying low. I quickly looked around. No one was in the waiting room. I strode across the room to the inner office door and again stayed beside it as I listened. I poked my head in and glanced around. It too appeared empty.

I crossed to the window and peeked out. Moonlight illuminated the street in an eerie gray gloom. I gazed up and down the block. A car drove by, its headlights cutting a white path in front of it. Then I noticed a dark figure standing near a tree across and down the street. He wore a dark overcoat and a fedora pulled down low. He appeared to be looking my way. Then he started down the sidewalk and disappeared around the corner. I watched for a minute longer, but he didn't reappear. I scrutinized the street again, and didn't see anything unusual.

I stepped over to my desk and flicked on a lamp. A soft glow lit the room. I looked around. A pen set that Clara had given me was on the edge of the desk where it was supposed to be. A small calendar as well. I opened the desk drawers and checked. That's when I noticed that the papers on top of my journal had been moved. I checked underneath them. The journal was still there. I went to the file cabinet and perused the files. Nothing appeared to be missing. I holstered my gun, tipped my hat back, and scratched my head. Why break in and not take anything? Was someone just looking for information? My journal notes tended to be cryptic, so there wouldn't be much to glean from them, but enough to know who I'd talked to and when. I went back to the waiting room, turned on a light, and then examined the door lock. It had been jimmied, which was why it hadn't been closed tightly. I'd have to get the landlord to fix it. I sighed. Another expense.

I walked back to my office and tossed my hat on the desk, then sat down. I leaned back in my chair and assessed things. I'd spooked someone. And that was a good thing. It meant I was on the right track. The problem was, I didn't know which track *was* the right one. The phone rang and brought me out of my reverie.

"It's Gordon Sandalwood. I was hoping you'd call me with an update. I've been trying to reach you all day." He sounded perturbed.

"I've been out, and I don't have any news yet," I said. "When I do, you'll be the first to know."

"Why do I get the feeling you're not telling me everything?"

Because I'm not, I wanted to say. But I didn't. "I'm close to something..." I glanced at the drawer where my journal was. "Give me a couple more days, and I'll explain everything."

He sighed audibly. "Okay," he said, disappointed.

I said goodbye and hung up, then picked up the phone again and dialed Chet.

"Dewey, old boy," Chet greeted me. I'd seen Chet in a bad mood before, and I'd seen him be as ruthless as an assassin, but he'd never been anything but friendly and cheerful toward me. And I was thankful for that. "How are things?"

"I talked to Fred Cooper."

"And?"

"He didn't deny the affair with Edith, but he says he's not blackmailing her."

"Of course he'd say that. What was your impression of him?"

"He's a cool customer, and he doesn't care about Edith or the child. He didn't ask me a thing about the boy. And he's hiding something." I explained how Cooper had reacted to questions about Edith's family, particularly Lester.

"Why would he care if you know that he knew Lester?" Chet asked. "He's not embarrassed by the affair. You think he's working with Lester to blackmail Edith?"

"Could be," I said. "I think I'll go by Lester's place and see if

I can get his neighbors to tell me about him. And if I can track him down, I might be able to rattle him enough that he'll slip up and tell me what he knows about Cooper."

"I wish I could give you more, but I can't find anything on Cooper. No criminal history, or trouble where he'd need a lawyer. He's clean. But you could talk to a guy I know who's out at Lowry."

"Who's that?"

"Sergeant Ray Parise. He's got a desk job at the base, and he knows a lot of people there. He's hesitant to talk to you because Cooper is a high-ranking officer, but I told him you know how to keep your mouth shut." He gave me the number and I wrote it down in my notepad. "He'll be working the day shift tomorrow if you want to call him."

"Thanks, Chet."

"Anytime. Sorry I wasn't more helpful."

"This is a start," I said. I swiveled around in my chair and looked out the window. "Shaking the tree is working, maybe too well."

"What happened?"

"Someone broke into my office today. They didn't take anything, but they looked through my paperwork."

"If you need any help from me, I'm a phone call away."

"Thanks," I said. "I'll let you know."

I hung up, and then tried Ray Parise. The phone rang and rang, and I finally put the receiver back in the cradle. He'd probably gone home for the night, so I'd have to try him again tomorrow. I got up, stretched, and went to the window to shut the blinds. And I thought I saw something move again. I shut the blinds slowly, still watching the street. Before the blinds closed completely, a shadow moved.

I left the lamp on, but walked out to the waiting room and into the hallway, which was dark. At the end of the hall was another window. I crept slowly toward it, careful to stay to the side. Then I gazed out and looked around. I counted to ten, and nothing happened. I was about to go back into the office when something small and red appeared across the street, next to another Victorian house that had been turned into offices. I squinted my eyes, and a minute later I saw it again. Someone was smoking a cigarette. What an amateur. One of the first things I'd learned in the army was not to smoke at night, or if you had to have a cigarette, to shield the end of it. Eventually I didn't see any more red glow, but periodically a shadow moved. Whatever dimwit was out there was watching my building.

I backed away from the window and returned to my office. I put on my hat and turned off the lamp, locked the inner office door, then walked in darkness into the hall and pulled that door closed. It didn't quite shut, but at this point, I wasn't worried about it. If that man outside had been in here, he'd seen whatever he'd wanted to. I pulled my gun out and tiptoed to the stairs, then eased down them. I crossed the foyer and looked out the front window. The man was still standing in the shadows across the street, still stupidly smoking his cigarette.

I hurried down the hall and out a back entrance that led into an alley behind the building. I ran down the alley toward Tenth and around the corner. A dog barked, and a car rolled by. I ducked to the right, trying to stay out of the glare of its headlights. I rushed across Sherman, past an old house on the corner, then stole down another alley, staying close to the side. I neared the building where the man had been standing, and I stopped and listened. Traffic hummed on the nearby streets. I raised my gun and peeked around the corner. The man was gone. I glanced all around, but didn't see any movement, so finally I walked to where he'd been and stared out into the street. He had disappeared. I squatted down and looked around, then noticed a few cigarette butts. Hand-rolled, just like the cigarette butts I'd found at Sonny's place. Coincidence? Or had the same man who'd been there been here?

I stood up and walked cautiously down Sherman. As I passed my office building, I looked around carefully. No one was there. I waited until I reached my car before I holstered my gun. I got in and drove slowly around the block, but I didn't see anyone. I spent a few minutes searching the neighborhood before I gave up. That man was long gone. Who was he? And how did he fit into blackmailing Edith?

I checked my watch. After eight. It was time to call it a day. But before I headed home, I was going to stop by Lester's place. He'd probably be out at a bar somewhere. Maybe I'd get lucky and catch him before he left.

CHAPTER TWENTY

As I turned onto Twentieth, the moon vanished behind clouds, leaving the street dark and eerie. I felt for my gun, then got out and strode purposefully toward Lester's apartment building. The bar on the corner was hopping, with people – mostly men – going in and out. The same loud blues music filled the street when the door opened.

I walked into the foyer. The lightbulb above the door barely lit a semicircle around me. I listened for a moment. A radio played somewhere. Then voices raised in anger. Something thumped and the voices stopped. I climbed the stairs to the third floor and stalked down the dark hallway to Lester's apartment. I rapped on the door and waited. Nothing happened, so I hit the door harder. I glanced over my shoulder, expecting Lester's neighbor to come out and yell at me.

The hallway was empty, so I tried the knob. It didn't budge. But it was a cheap knob, so I pulled out a pocketknife, flicked open a thin blade, and slid it between the door and the jamb. I wiggled it around a bit and felt the latch give. I pushed the door open, slipped inside, and shut it quietly behind me. I locked it, then closed and pocketed the knife. A powerful odor hit me, a mixture of sweat and stale cigarettes. I ignored it. The moon had come back out and I let my eyes adjust. A rectangular window directly across from me was covered by curtains, but a slice of ghostly light seeped around the edges. I strained to hear anything. Silence. I waited a moment and then felt along the wall until I found a light switch. I flicked it on.

A single bulb in the center of the ceiling didn't do much to light the small room, but there wasn't much to see. Against one dingy wall was a cheap couch, its stuffing protruding from tears in the worn fabric. A tattered blanket lay crumpled up on one end of it. Two empty whiskey bottles were toppled on the floor next to the couch. Against the opposite wall was a wood table with a cheap radio, some pieces of paper and a small book lying on it. A single metal chair sat close by.

On the other side of the table was an archway. I stepped toward it and saw a pair of boots on the floor. I drew my gun, moved to the wall next to the archway, and listened. Nothing, so I poked my head around the corner...and found Lester.

He was lying on his side on the floor of a minuscule kitchenette. A pool of blood spread out beneath him. His mouth was open and his dead eyes stared at the wall. The room was full of shadows, so I pulled a chain to turn on an overhead light, then stepped carefully over to him and crouched down, careful to stay out of the blood. The front of his plaid shirt was stained dark, and one of his hands was clutched over his stomach. Dried blood covered the hand. I looked more closely and noticed that his shirt had a few cuts in it. I reached out and gingerly pulled at the fabric around one of the tears. The blood on his shirt was dry and crusty. I carefully undid a couple of buttons until I could see the wound. It was a small slash, definitely from a knife. Someone had stabbed Lester and he'd bled to death. The dried blood told me he'd been dead for quite a while.

I gingerly buttoned the shirt again, sighed, stood up and surveyed the kitchen. A few filthy dishes were in a grime-stained sink. Grease was spattered on an old stove. Another whiskey bottle sat on a dirty counter, along with two empty shot glasses. I went to a refrigerator and opened it. It was empty except for a half-full bottle of milk. The cupboards were nearly bare as well, just a few cans of beans and a box of crackers. I didn't know what I had hoped to find, so I wasn't disappointed.

I stepped back across Lester, slipped into the main room and glanced around. Nothing in the apartment indicated that Lester had struggled with someone, so he probably knew his murderer. Had that person sat at the couch and shared a drink with Lester, and when Lester wasn't looking, stabbed him? I walked to the couch and felt between the cushions, but didn't find anything. I turned around.

Near the table was a door. I strode over and opened it. Inside hung two pairs of dirty pants and a few shirts. There were no other doors in the apartment, so I assumed bathrooms were somewhere down the hall. I closed the closet door and my eyes fell to the table. I moved quietly over and picked up one of the pieces of paper.

A list of items was on it: $50 gold slug, 1870-S silver dollar, 1880 dime. Next to each one was a figure. The figures ranged from a few dollars up to a thousand. I totaled the list. It was close to fifty thousand dollars. I picked up another piece of paper. It had Fred Cooper's name written on it. Did that mean Lester *knew* of Cooper or had he actually *met* Cooper? Had Cooper lied about knowing Lester? I dropped the papers and picked up the book. *A Guide to Coin Collecting*. Lester had been educating himself on coin collecting. And it didn't take a genius to know that Lester'd had his eye on John Norland's coin collection. But how did Lester know so much about it? Had Norland or Ruby talked to Lester before he had died?

I set the book down and glanced back at Lester's body. Had someone killed him because of old coins or for some other reason? And then I remembered what Chet had said about Sonny O'Hara: he liked to use a knife. Maybe one of the neighbors had seen something. I pulled out my notepad and quickly jotted down the figures on the paper. I was tempted to steal the paper, but I didn't really want to tamper with evidence the police could use. Once I finished, I stuffed the notepad back in my pocket. I started for the door, then remembered that the apartment was now a crime scene, so I pulled a handkerchief from my pocket and spent a few minutes wiping off the surfaces that I'd touched. When I finished, I went to the door and was about to open it when loud voices erupted from the other side. I froze. The voices sounded like they were near the top of the stairs.

"I told you not to go there," a shrill female voice yelled. "And you were looking at her!"

"I was not," a deep male voice shouted back. "And what were you doing there?"

"Looking for you!"

"Swell. I can't even have a drink without you coming around."

I didn't know the voices. I stood by the door and waited. The argument continued, but they didn't leave the hallway. I gritted my teeth. Then a knock on Lester's door startled me.

"Lester! You in there?"

I *did* recognize this voice. It was the neighbor who lived

across the hall. He pounded on the door again. I swore I could smell booze seeping between the cracks in the door.

"Hey, man, you owe me ten bucks. Lester, open up."

He must've seen the light on and assumed Lester was home. I thought about the body in the kitchen. Lester was home, but he'd never entertain guests again. The argument down the hall continued. I thought the neighbor had moved away, but then the knob rattled. I quickly moved to the side of the door and got out my gun. The knob jiggled again, but didn't give. Then he smacked on the door a third time.

"Are you ignoring me? Fine. I'll be down at the bar. If you don't have the full ten, bring me what you got, okay?"

Footsteps faded, but the argument between the couple was still in full force. I didn't want to wait around, so I shut off the lights and tiptoed to the window. I pulled back the curtains and looked out. A small landing was attached to a fire escape that led down to an alley below. I opened the latch and raised the window, using my handkerchief to prevent fingerprints, then poked my head out and looked around. The sounds of traffic on Larimer filtered up to me, but no one was in the alley.

I glanced over my shoulder. The argument in the hall had intensified, so I climbed out onto the landing, closed the window and started down the fire escape. I had to stop once when a teenager cut through the alley. He had no clue I was above him, and once he was gone, I continued to the bottom of the fire escape. I had to drop six feet down to the ground and lost my hat in the process. I groped around in the dark until I found it, and brushed it off as I strode around to the front of the building.

Then something dawned on me. I'd touched the hallway doorknob to Lester's apartment. I shook my head, then stole back inside, stood in the foyer and listened. The couple who'd been arguing were gone, and it was now deathly silent. I ran up to the third floor and down the empty hall to Lester's door. I quickly wiped off the doorknob, pocketed my handkerchief and dashed back downstairs and outside. The blues music emanated from the bar on the corner. I'd place money on that being where Lester's neighbor had gone. I put on my hat and walked toward it.

CHAPTER TWENTY-ONE

When I strolled through the door, loud, raucous voices, laughter, and cigarette smoke assailed me. The place was crowded, with people standing around high tables and at a long wooden bar across from the door. Others were packed into booths. A jukebox in the corner blared "Baby, It's Cold Outside" by Louis Jordan and Ella Fitzgerald. I was overdressed in my suit and tie, as most of the clientele wore uniforms and other work clothes, but not suits. I endured stares as I scanned the patrons. I spotted a man with thinning red hair seated at a stool near the end of the bar. I edged my way between tables and sidled up to him. I gestured at the bartender and ordered a shot of scotch, then glanced at the red-haired man. He was a bloated fifty, with sunken eyes and sallow skin. His arms lacked muscle and he held a beer mug with puffy hands. He'd long since gone soft, his only exertion the lifting of that beer mug.

The bartender returned with my shot. I paid for it, threw it back and set the glass down. Then I turned to my red-haired neighbor. "You know Lester Klassen." It was a statement and my look dared him to deny it.

He surveyed me, took a swig of his beer and wiped the back of his hand across his mouth. "Yeah, so?"

"I need to ask you about him."

His eyes darted around and then he considered me carefully. "You a cop?"

I shook my head and pulled a ten from my wallet. He saw the Colt and his eyes grew wide.

He held up his hands. "I don't want any trouble, you hear?"

"Lester owes you ten bucks. I'll pay you the ten for a little information about him."

He eyed the money greedily, then reached out for it.

I waved the bill at him. "You want the money, start talking."

"All right," he muttered.

"What's your name?"

"I don't want no trouble, mister." I glared at him. "It's Norman Dewitt."

"How long have you known Lester?" I began.

He gulped some beer, then said, "About six months. That's when he moved in across the hall."

"What's he like?"

"He's a loud mouth, thinks he knows everything. I mostly drink with him. He's got an ex-wife somewhere and he says she owes him money. But that's not the way it is with Lester. *He* owes people money."

"Like you."

He grimaced. "And practically everyone else."

That sounded like what I'd heard of Lester.

Norman waved the bartender over. "Hey, Mike, does Lester owe you money?"

The bartender ambled over. "What's that?" he said over the jukebox.

I pointed at Norman. "He says Lester Klassen owes you money."

"Is snow white?" Mike said. "Of course he does, and I told him the last time he was in here that he wasn't getting another drop out of me until he paid."

"When was that?" I asked.

Mike shrugged, then said, "A week ago."

"Did you talk to him much?" I went on.

He threw me a wry look. "Once Lester gets drinking, you can't shut him up."

"What'd he say?"

He shrugged again. "The usual stuff. How everyone is against him."

"I've heard that before," Norman said.

"Yeah," Mike continued. "Although lately, he's changed his tune."

"How so?" I asked.

"Now it's how he's going to score big and then his problems will be over, and we'll all be sorry for giving him a hard time."

"What big money?"

Mike laughed. "Beats me. All I know is I told him if he couldn't pay for his drinks, then he better get lost. So he left, and he stiffed me."

Someone hollered his name, so Mike ambled down to the other end of the bar.

I turned back to Norman. "Has Lester been in any kind of trouble lately?"

He snorted. "He's got gambling debts."

"Would anyone that he owes hurt him?"

"I don't know. Maybe he crossed the wrong person."

"Where does Lester work?"

"He gets odd jobs around town, but since I've known him, he's never had anything steady. I think he steals for what little money he gets."

"Has his ex-wife ever come around?" I described Ruby.

"Never seen her."

"What about another woman with blond hair? Her name is Edith."

He shook his head. "They'd be foolish to come into this neighborhood."

"Have you seen a guy with brown hair and a mustache? Likes to wear a black coat and a pork pie hat? Name's Sonny O'Hara."

He shook his head again.

"What about a big guy, not too tall, with slicked-back hair?"

He glanced around. "Sounds like half the guys in here."

I thought for a moment. "So no strangers in your building."

"Not since you woke me up this morning." He guffawed, but then grew serious. "Now that you mention it, there was a guy that came around Lester's place a time or two in the last few weeks."

"What'd he look like?"

He scrutinized me. "Kind of like you."

"Me?"

"Yeah. Tall, clean cut. Didn't look like he belonged in this neighborhood."

Fred Cooper? I wondered.

"Anything else?" I asked. "Did this clean-cut guy smoke cigarettes? Did he roll his own?"

"I dunno. I just saw him go into Lester's apartment. That's it."

"Did Lester ever talk to you about coins or selling coins?"

"Coins?" He wrinkled his nose at me. "Are you kidding me? If Lester ever had any spare change, he'd be spending it here."

"Did he ever talk about going to Limon?"

"Hell, I don't know." He lifted his mug. "I told you, we drink and I don't pay that much attention to anything he says." He swigged some more beer.

I held up a hand. "Okay." I let him drink a bit, and then said, "Have the police ever been around?"

"All the time, but not at Lester's place." He swiveled on his stool so that he faced me squarely. "What are you getting at?"

"Nothing," I said. "I just need to find him."

"Well, he ain't here." He guffawed again at his joke. "Now how about that dough?"

I handed him the ten. "Thanks for your time."

He smiled crookedly. "This'll do just fine." Then he downed the last of his beer and shook the empty mug at Mike to indicate he wanted another.

I squeezed between tables to a hallway where bathrooms were located. There was also a pay phone. I fed in a nickel and dialed the operator. Over the sound of the music, I barely heard her answer.

"Police," I barked into the phone.

She connected me and a moment later, a deep male voice said, "Sergeant McCleary."

"There's a dead guy in apartment 302, on Twentieth Street." I rattled off the address, and before he could ask anything else, I hung up.

I walked back to my car, thinking about Lester lying on the floor in his kitchen. He'd wanted to score big, most likely from John Norland's coin collection. Lester had scored all right, but it hadn't been what he was expecting.

CHAPTER TWENTY-TWO

Clara was in bed when I got home, but she wasn't asleep. She'd been worrying again, and she didn't relax until I was in bed beside her. I held her close and she finally fell asleep. I stared at the ceiling for a long time before I drifted off into a slumber that was filled with dreams of dead bodies, both those long gone and some more recent, including Lester.

Saturday arrived with a chilly storm that brought snow flurries. I'd slept a little later than usual and ate breakfast with Clara. I finished my coffee and checked my watch. Just after eight o'clock. I picked up the phone and called Ray Parise at Lowry. I identified myself and he quickly lowered his voice.

"I know who you are," he said. "I can't talk now. Can you meet me near Quebec and Fifth. There's a field on the west side of the street. Park there and we can talk. I'll come on my lunch hour. 12:10."

"I'll be there."

I hung up and dialed Ruby Klassen. Sam was in a bassinet near the table, and I glanced down at him and smiled. He blinked at me with big brown eyes.

"Hello?" Ruby answered after a few rings.

"It's Dewey Webb."

"What's going on? Have you found out anything?"

"A thing or two. Have the police talked to you?"

She sucked in a breath. "The police? What for?"

They hadn't gotten to her yet, which meant I'd be the one to deliver the news about Lester.

"I need to talk to you and Edith together," I said. "Can you call her and get her to come to your house without it seeming suspicious?"

"I can call right now. Edith sometimes comes over on Saturdays, so it won't seem unusual."

"Good. See if you can arrange it and call me back." I gave her the number.

"What's this about?"

"All in good time," I said.

"Fine. I'll talk to Edith and call you back."

I hung up, then picked up Sam while I waited.

"It seems like he grows stronger every day," I said to Clara.

She was doing dishes and she turned around. "He's growing like a weed; isn't that what they say?"

Sam grabbed my finger and held on. "My, aren't you strong?" I wiggled my finger and he held on. I felt eyes on me and glanced up. Clara was watching us, her face tired, but also soft and warm. "What?" I asked.

She smiled. "Nothing."

The phone rang and Sam jumped and then burst into tears. Clara rushed over and took him from me. "Oh Sam, it's nothing," she cooed at him.

"Sorry," I said.

"Don't worry about it." She went into the other room while I answered.

"Edith can be here in half an hour," Ruby said.

"Good. I'll be there, too."

"Are you going to tell me what's going on?"

"I'll tell both of you at once."

She sighed. "Okay. I'll see you soon."

I hung up and went into the living room. Clara was sitting on the couch with Sam. He'd quieted down and was cooing again. I leaned down and kissed him, and then her. I sat down next to her and shared the barest details about my case. I chose, however, not to tell her about the man I'd seen outside my office last night, or about Lester.

After a few minutes, I checked my watch. "I've got to go out," I said.

She nodded. "I know. You think you're making progress?"

"Some." I put on my overcoat and hat. "I'll get to the bottom of this soon, and then we'll go dancing."

"I'm holding you to that."

I kept her smile in my mind as I walked out the door.

———

Twenty minutes later, I was back in the Baker neighborhood, sitting in the overstuffed chair in Ruby's living room. Ruby and Edith sat next to each other on the loveseat. A small oil heater in the corner did a serviceable job of warming the room.

"So." Edith was wearing a simple print dress and her face was artfully made up, but it couldn't hide the apprehension in her eyes. She put her hands in her lap and fixed an expectant gaze at me. "What's going on that I had to rush over here?"

"Gordon wasn't suspicious?" I asked.

"Probably," she said. "I told him I'd already made plans to come over and I'd forgotten to tell him."

Ruby pointed at me. "Quit stalling."

I still hesitated, then said, "Lester's dead."

Ruby's hands covered her mouth. "No!"

Edith stared at me. "What happened?"

I told them about finding him, but I left out the part about breaking in, and I suppose they were shocked enough that they didn't ask.

"He was stabbed?" Ruby whispered when I finished.

I nodded. Ruby stared out the window for a long moment. A few small snowflakes fell onto her tiny brown lawn. Edith reached over and squeezed her hand.

"It's funny," Ruby said. "I don't care about him anymore, and yet..." her voice trailed off.

"Who would do this?" Edith asked.

"Nobody really liked him," Ruby said. "But I don't know why anyone would want to kill him."

I pulled out my notepad and flipped it open, then showed it to them. "I think Lester was after your father's coin collection."

Ruby took the notepad from me and read it, her finger tapping her mouth thoughtfully. "How did he know so much about the coins?"

"Did Dad talk to him about it?" Edith asked.

Ruby shrugged. "It's possible. It wasn't a big secret that Dad collected coins, but I don't know if anybody thought there was any value in them."

"There's one thing I don't get," I said. I gestured at Ruby. "If you have the collection, and someone knows about it, why not just steal the coins from you? Why try and blackmail Edith?"

"Because the collection isn't here," Ruby said. "I put it in a safety deposit box."

Edith stared at her. "You did?"

Ruby nodded. "Well, not all of it. There are bags of pennies and nickels I have around here, but I took a lot of the higher denomination coins to the bank."

"That makes sense," I said.

Then Ruby gasped.

"What?" I asked.

"Now that you mention it, I think someone did break in a while back. I was never sure because nothing was taken. But I could've sworn someone had been in the house. I thought it was Lester, trying to look for any cash I might have lying around. Which I don't." She let out a small laugh. "I don't have anything valuable here. It didn't occur to me that he – or someone – might be after the coin collection."

"If they were searching for the collection and didn't find it, they didn't bother with anything else," I said.

"But what about the smaller coins?" Edith asked.

"That's not where the big money is," I said. "Someone broke in and didn't find the coins they expected to, so they're trying to blackmail Edith to get it."

I pointed to the notepad. "Is that list accurate?"

Ruby studied it. "I don't really know. I never paid much attention to what Dad had, but he did tell me that after he was gone, I should either sell the coins or get a safety deposit box for them. I thought he was being a little dramatic about it, but after he passed and I moved here, I decided I'd get a box for them because I didn't want to hassle with selling them. And I thought that, if I held onto them, some of them might gain value over time."

"I'll duplicate that list," I said. "Can you go to the bank and check to see if your dad had the coins on the list?"

She nodded. "I'll go first thing Monday."

"How long had your father been collecting?" I asked.

"A long time." Ruby ran a hand over the notepad. "I wonder if these figures are correct."

"If that list of coins reflects some of what your father had, it looks like there might be a whole lot of coins that are valuable," I said. "I'm going to visit the coin shop to talk to the proprietor.

He might know more about your father's collection and,"–I took the notepad back from Ruby–"whether Lester or anyone else has come in to talk to him about selling some of those coins Lester had written down."

"But I still don't understand why someone would want to kill Lester," Ruby said.

"If he was trying to blackmail Edith, he was working with someone." I started to write down Lester's figures on another sheet of paper.

"What about Sonny O'Hara?" Edith asked.

I glanced up at her. "I'll be paying him a visit, too. But from what he said to you, he's only been hired to help in all this. Unless he got wind of the coin collection and knocked off Lester so he could have the coins for himself." I continued writing, but turned the conversation in a different direction. "And I don't know about the Pattersons. Did they know about the collection?"

"You still think they might have something to do with this?" Edith asked.

I shrugged. "They took money from you once, and asked for more. Raising a child is costly. I can't eliminate them just yet. And Ralph Patterson may have been around town in the last couple of days."

"So?" Ruby asked.

"Someone was watching my office last night, and this gent may have been talking to Sonny, too. Whoever he is, he rolls his own smokes. And Ralph rolls his own cigarettes." She started to protest and I held up a hand to stop her. "I know, a lot of people roll their own, but I have to consider Ralph as well. The Pattersons need money, they knew about Edith – obviously – and after I talked to Gladys' sister Thelma, she could've warned them I was asking around..."

"And Ralph decided to try to scare you off," Edith finished.

I cocked my eyebrows. "It's possible. Or he's worried that I might report that they have Gerry and he's coming after me for that."

Ruby shook her head. "Thelma Blanchard called me after you talked to her. She was upset that you were asking questions."

"It couldn't be helped," I said.

"She said she talked to Gladys and Ralph as well," Ruby went on. "They haven't left Vernon. And they're upset about all this. They just want to be able to raise Gerry in peace."

"Thelma could be covering for them." I pursed my lips. "Is there any way they knew about your father's coin collection?"

"A lot of people could've known," Edith said. "Dad was a local doctor. He knew just about everyone in town."

Ruby crossed her arms. "I doubt the Pattersons ever went to a doctor. They couldn't have afforded it. So they wouldn't have known Dad, and I don't see how they'd have known about his coin collection."

"Thelma said she thought Lester stole from your father," I said. "Did he steal any of your father's coins?"

"It's entirely possible," Ruby said. "Lester couldn't be trusted at all."

"There's something else." I turned to Edith. "I found a piece of paper along with the list of coins. It had Fred Cooper's name on it."

It was Edith's turn to gasp. "What? Lester knew Fred?"

"It looks that way," I said.

"You think Fred's trying to blackmail me?" Edith asked. "Does he need the money?"

I shrugged. "I don't know, but I think it's possible."

"Oh, Lester is nothing but a —" Ruby didn't finish the sentence.

Edith grimaced.

155

"Did Cooper know about the collection?" I asked her.

"I doubt I ever mentioned it to him," Edith said. "It's not something you talk about when you're in love."

I nodded. "Did he know Lester back then?"

"Fred never met any of my family," she said.

"But did you *talk* about your family?"

"I'm sure I did. Why?"

"I talked to Fred, and he first said you may have mentioned your family, but you didn't discuss them."

"I'm sure I did, at least a time or two."

I nodded. "It looks like Fred knows – knew – Lester, and he's lying about it."

"Why?" Ruby asked.

"He'd lie if he was blackmailing me," Edith said wryly.

"Right," I said. "But if he is behind this, he's risking a lot. He's fairly high up in the Air Force now."

"How will you find out if he's doing this to Edith?" Ruby asked.

I finished with the list, tore the paper off, and handed it to Ruby. "I'm not sure. But I'm going to revisit Cooper."

Edith let out a little moan. "I hope you find whoever's behind this. I'm running out of time."

"We'll know soon," I said with more confidence than I felt. I hadn't been able to eliminate any suspects so far.

Ruby squeezed Edith's hands. "He'll figure it out."

I pocketed my notepad and stood up. "Ladies, thanks for your time. Edith, I'll give you a call later. If Gordon answers, I'll hang up, wait a few minutes and call again. Try and pick up, okay?"

"I can do that," she said.

I tipped my hat at them. They were still sitting on the loveseat in stunned silence when I let myself out.

CHAPTER TWENTY-THREE

I left Ruby's house and headed straight to Lipan Street. When I drove up to Sonny O'Hara's apartment building, three young hoods were loitering near the door. They all wore jeans with the cuffs rolled up, black leather jackets, and white T-shirts. I got out and walked toward them, bracing myself for trouble.

"Man, you got a light?" one of them asked me as I passed. His light-brown hair fell onto his forehead, only partially covering a thin scar above one eyebrow. He had a cigarette in one hand, but his other hand was down by his side. His two buddies placed themselves on either side of me. They puffed up their chests, but neither one was big enough to be truly intimidating.

I paused and stared at them. "Sure." As I pulled out my lighter, I backed up slightly to take them all in. I flicked open the lighter, and as I held my hand out, I made sure my coat fell open so they'd see the Colt in its holster. Brown-hair stiffened, but kept his cool. He subtly signaled the others with his eyes and they each took a step back.

"Thanks, man." Brown-hair lifted his hand, lit his cigarette, and blew smoke away from me.

"No problem," I said. "It's a cold day to be outside."

"We're waitin' for someone," Brown-hair said.

I nodded, then left them and strolled inside with a grin on my face. Punks. The hall was still, not even the landlady's music emanating from behind her door. I dashed up the stairs, turned the corner, and strode up to Sonny's door. I banged on it and waited. When nothing happened, I knocked again, but still no Sonny. I gave it to the count of ten, then went back downstairs and knocked on the landlady's door. She didn't answer either, so I hurried back outside. The three hoods were still loitering near the door.

"Have you seen Sonny O'Hara?" I asked the brown-haired one.

"Nah, man, he hasn't been around for a couple of days," he said. "He sometimes sleeps somewhere else."

If Sonny had killed Lester, it made sense that he was laying low for a while.

My gun had apparently made Brown-hair cooperative. "Where?" I asked.

"Beats me, I just know he isn't here."

"Is he in some kind of trouble?" I asked, thinking maybe he'd heard something.

He shrugged. "Like everyone else around here."

His pals snickered, but he glowered at them and they stopped.

The brown-haired kid seemed to be their leader, so I threw him a hard glare. "Have you seen Sonny with a big guy with dark hair that's slicked back?"

He glanced away, suddenly reserved.

I shifted to make sure he saw the gun again. "Has that guy been around here?"

"Yeah," he finally said. "The other day."

"Do you know his name?"

He hesitated, then said sullenly, "Don't know."

I grabbed his arm and pushed him against the side of the building. He wasn't expecting it, nor was he as tough as he thought he was, and he caved in.

"Boyd Schuler," he said.

I'd never heard of him. "Did you hear him talking with Sonny?"

He shook his head. The other two kept silent.

"I just saw them talking, that's it," Brown-hair said hurriedly. "I don't know anything else."

I'd scared him, and he wasn't going to lie again. "Thanks."

"You don't want to mess with Schuler," he said.

"I'll keep that in mind." I hurried to my car and left.

———

On my way to the coin shop, I took a chance and stopped by the law offices of Masters and O'Reilly. It was a little after nine and the door was unlocked, so I let myself in. Miriam Malloy wasn't working, and the lobby was empty and quiet. Then I heard a voice down the hall.

"Chet?" I called out.

"In here," came his soft tenor voice.

I strolled down the hall to his office. He was just hanging up the phone, and he waved me in. His desk faced the door, not the gorgeous view of the snowcapped Rocky Mountains through the window behind him. Typical of him, to focus on the task at hand.

"You're working?" he asked.

I took a seat at an oak chair that sat in front of his small metal desk. "As are you."

"I've got a case that's keeping me going day and night," he said.

I let my eyes rove around his office. It was nothing more than functional, with numerous file cabinets and bracketed shelves that had nothing on them but a few newspapers. No signs of his personal life.

He leaned back in his chair and surveyed me. "What's on your mind?"

"I finally got the name of the mysterious stranger who's been hanging around with Sonny O'Hara."

"Oh yeah?"

"Boyd Schuler."

He nodded. "I've heard of him. He got pinched a while back for burglary, did a fair stint for it."

I cocked an eyebrow. "Did you pinch him?"

Chet's lips twitched into a faint smile. "Yeah." He rubbed his chin thoughtfully. "So he's back out on the streets."

"Afraid so," I said. "What do you know about him?"

"He's smarter than Sonny O'Hara, that's for sure, and he's always looking to score. He's been in and out of jail since he was a teenager, always seems to find trouble."

"How old is he now?"

"Let me see, by now, about thirty, I'd guess." He stood up and went to one of the filing cabinets, opened it, and took out a file. He came back to the desk and handed it to me. "There's what I have on him."

The file was thin, with only a few notes. Schuler was born March 3, 1916, which made him thirty-three. He'd been in and out of orphanages since he was five, and had been arrested for vagrancy, burglary and other petty crimes. A mug shot in the file showed dark, mean eyes, the slicked-back hair that everyone mentioned, a square jaw, and a crooked nose. He'd been in a fight or two.

"A face only a mother could love," I said. I closed the file and slid it across the desk.

"Yeah." Chet gazed at me. "Have you figured out how Schuler and Sonny O'Hara are connected to the girls you're helping?"

"I don't know yet, but someone's after a coin collection that may be quite valuable. Only problem is the collection is in a safety deposit box, so it can't be stolen outright."

"So someone blackmails the girls, knowing they'll sell the coins for cash," he said.

I nodded, then pointed at the file. "Boyd's last known address is old. Any idea how I might find him?"

"He used to spend his nights around the bars on Larimer," he said. "But that's been years ago."

"Nice area," I said sarcastically. "I can run by there tonight and see if anyone's seen him around. A Saturday night, should be busy."

"Be careful."

"I will. Anything else you remember about Schuler?"

"He had a rough upbringing, and he doesn't trust anyone." He tapped his fingertips together for a moment, then said, "I wouldn't have given Sonny or Boyd the brains to cook up a scheme like that."

"I don't think they did." I gestured out the window. The snow had stopped. "How could Sonny or Boyd have known about Edith's situation? Neither one of them is from Limon, and I doubt either one visits there. Someone had to have told them, or, as Sonny said to Edith, he's just the middleman and he doesn't know anything about the coins." I paused.

Chet pierced me with an inquisitive gaze. "What?"

"I've got another problem." I told him about Lester's murder.

"He knew about the coin collection?" he asked.

"It looks that way. Lester's a lowlife, so I could see him crossing paths with Sonny and Boyd. If Lester's the one black-mailing Edith, he would need to hire someone to meet her for the money exchange, because he couldn't go himself or she'd turn him in."

Chet rested his chin on his hands and thought about it. "The only problem is, I don't see Sonny committing murder. Frankly, he's not that tough."

"What about Schuler?" I asked.

He mulled that over. "More possible, I suppose, but he's never assaulted anyone before. At least not that I'm aware of."

"Which leads me to another theory," I said. "Fred Cooper's name was written on a piece of paper in Lester's apartment, and Lester's neighbor said he saw a man who might fit Cooper's description at Lester's apartment a couple of times in the last few weeks. But Cooper said he doesn't know Lester."

"Fred Cooper's the one Edith had the affair with." It was a statement; Chet didn't forget anything.

"Yes. What if Lester and Colonel Cooper both knew about the coins, and they knew each other, and they devised a plan together to blackmail Edith, knowing she had access to these coins that she could sell. The colonel is the brains, and Lester brings in the thugs to get the money from Edith."

"That's a lot of 'what-if's," he said.

I held up my hands in surrender. "I didn't say I had it all figured out."

He smiled. "But then Lester got greedy and Cooper knocked him off."

"Unless Sonny or Boyd killed Lester so they wouldn't have to split the dough with him."

"Have you talked to Sonny?"

I shook my head. "I stopped by his place, but he wasn't there, and no one's seen him for a while. I thought I'd see what you had on Schuler, and then I'm going to stop at the coin shop to see if Colonel Cooper or Lester have been asking about John Norland's coin collection. After that, I'm headed to the base to talk to your friend about Colonel Cooper. Maybe he can shed some light on why a colonel in the Air Force might need money so badly he'd resort to blackmail."

"And then you nail Colonel Cooper for lying to you."

"Something like that. And if I need to, I find Schuler and talk to him."

Chet flashed a smile. "Your dance card is full today."

I nodded. "I just hope it leads to a murderer."

"Speaking of that," he said. "Did you report Lester's murder?"

"Anonymously. I didn't want to spend the night explaining why I'd broken into his apartment, and then get caught up in red tape. If that happened, I'd never find who's doing this to Edith."

He nodded. "If I hear anything through the grapevine, I'll let you know."

"Thanks." I stood up to go.

He was back on the phone before I reached the door.

CHAPTER TWENTY-FOUR

"May I help you?" the owner asked when I walked into Denver Stamp and Coin. He was sitting at his desk behind the display cases, his glasses perched on his nose, and a magnifying glass held in one hand. In the other he was holding a stamp with a pair of tweezers.

"I hope so," I said. I strode to the back. A faint musty odor permeated the room, reminding me of the attic in the house I grew up in. "I was in here the other day."

He gently set the stamp down in a plastic container and set the magnifying glass aside. "I just bought a rare stamp from Spain," he said with more enthusiasm than I could ever muster up for a stamp. He pushed himself up and came slowly around the desk, then leaned against the display case. "You were in here recently?" He furrowed his brow. He obviously didn't remember me.

"I talked to you about a woman who sold a St. Gaudens to you, and about John Norland from Limon, and his coin collection."

"Ah, yes." He took off his glasses and waited expectantly.

I pulled out my wallet and flashed my PI license at him. "Could you tell me more about the collection?"

"What's this about?"

"Just trying to track down some information," I said easily.

"I see." He leaned his hands on the counter and thought. "I'm not sure what all Mr. Norland had in his collection when he died. We'd talk about various coins, not just the ones he owned, but ones he wanted to obtain." His British accent grew thicker the more he talked.

"Did he buy just from you?"

"No. It's easy to purchase by mail-order, so John bought and sold things that way, as well as coming in here."

"Did he ever talk about the value of his collection?"

"We discussed it a time or two, but coins gain and lose value over time. I'd have to know what's in a collection before I could speculate on what it was worth."

I pretended to study the coins in the case. What was I missing?

"Has a man about my height, with light hair in a military buzz, come in here lately?" I finally asked.

He mulled that over. "No, I don't think so."

"What about a really thin guy with brown hair? And knowing him, he would've smelled like he'd been drinking."

He chuckled. "That's not the kind of clientele I get."

"Has anyone been asking about John Norland's collection?"

A sly grin formed on his lips. "Besides you?"

"Right." I returned the smile.

"No, only you. Why the interest in Norland's collection?"

I winked at him. "I'm working on that." I turned to go.

"There is one thing," he said. I whirled around. "I almost hate to mention it. It could be nothing."

"Anything's helpful."

"I do know that Norland had at least a few St. Gaudens. He

told me he picked them up from a dealer in San Francisco a long time ago."

"And?"

"A gentleman came in about a week ago, and he was asking about pieces like that, what their value was and would I be interested in buying them."

"What'd he look like?"

He glanced away, embarrassed. "I didn't pay that much attention." Then he closed his eyes. "He was taller, with...gray hair, so maybe he was a little older." His eyelids flew open and he stared at me. "He was a pretty ordinary-looking man."

I frowned. That didn't sound like any of my suspects. "Do you remember how he was dressed?"

"A suit and tie, like most people who come in here."

"Did he give you a name?"

He shook his head. "No, there wouldn't be any reason for him to."

"Did he ask about any other coins?"

"No, just the St. Gaudens." His shoulders lifted up in the slightest of shrugs.

"Would you purchase the coins from him?"

"If we could agree on the price, then yes, as long as they weren't stolen."

"How would you know if they were stolen?"

He shrugged. "Sometimes the police will inform dealers of items that have been stolen."

"Did he buy anything?"

Another shake of his head. "I'm sorry I couldn't be more helpful," he said, his tone dismissive. The questioning was over.

"I appreciate your time," I said. This time I did leave.

———

On my way out to Lowry Air Force Base, I thought about what the shop owner had said. If Lester or Cooper had been researching old coins, they'd gone somewhere else for their information. And now I had a new wrinkle, in the gray-haired man. I had no idea who he was, or if he meant anything to my case. These thoughts rattled around in my brain as I listened to Duke Ellington on the radio. Light snow had started falling again, and it hit my windshield and melted into tiny water droplets.

At exactly ten after twelve, I was parked at the field near Quebec and Fifth. Since Ray Parise was in the military, I assumed he would be punctual. Sure enough, just as I parked the Plymouth, a white Ford pulled into the field. A man in a blue garrison cap drove up right beside my car, driver-side door to driver-side door. He gestured at me and we both rolled down our windows. He kept his car running and put his hands in front of the heating vent to warm them.

"Dewey Webb?" he asked.

"Yes," I said. "Thanks for meeting me."

Parise gave me a quick once-over, so I gave him one as well. He looked to be in his mid-twenties, with hair the color of walnuts, a chubby face, and languid eyes that made him look as if he'd just rolled out of bed.

"Chet says I can trust you," he said.

"You have my word, this conversation stays here."

"What'd Chet tell you about me?"

"Nothing. Just that you might have some information on Colonel Cooper."

Sergeant Parise nodded. "I owe Chet. He saved my life during the war."

It was typical of Chet to not tell me that. "Chet's solid," I said. "And he said whatever we talk about stays here."

"It wouldn't do me any good to tell anyone, but yeah, you can trust me."

I noticed he didn't even ask why I wanted to know about Colonel Cooper, which was exactly what I wanted.

He studied me hard. "I've only got a few minutes before I need to get back." He pointed through his windshield toward the base. "I need enough time to eat lunch."

"I appreciate you meeting me."

He glanced in his rearview mirror. "I'm taking a risk. If Colonel Cooper found out I was talking about him, it'd be bad." He smoothed the front of his blue jacket and adjusted his cap, as if an officer might see him and call him out on the neatness of his appearance.

I got right to it. "Tell me about him."

"There's not much to tell. He's a colonel, right?" I nodded. "So he's got a lot of say around the base." There was a negative edge in his tone.

"You don't like him," I said.

He hesitated. "No."

"Why not?"

"He's arrogant and thinks the world revolves around him. He lit into me a time or two for things I didn't even do wrong."

"Officers," I said, commiserating with his predicament.

He nodded. "He's not very popular around the base."

"Has he been acting unusual lately?"

"I wouldn't say unusual..." He stopped to light a cigarette. He blew smoke out the window, then said, "I work in the same area as he does. I'm an assistant to another officer. The day before yesterday, Colonel Cooper came storming out of his office, mad as a wet hen. He yelled to his secretary, and said not to let that Buster bother him again. Does that mean anything to you?"

"I don't know," I said noncommittally. "He said 'Buster'?"

He nodded. "Whoever had called him really got his goat. He was angry the rest of the day. No one wanted to cross paths with him."

"When did he get that call? Morning or afternoon?"

"It was in the morning."

"Is he in some kind of trouble?"

"Not that I've heard of."

"Does he gamble?"

"I don't think so. There are some weekly poker nights. Guys like to talk about their cards, and who the big winners and losers are, which guys are good, and the ones that stink. I've never heard anyone talk about him."

"Any issues with money?"

He shook his head.

"Any rumors about him playing around on his wife, something like that?" I said it casually, just part of the conversation.

"No, he's married." Then he snickered. "I guess that wouldn't stop him, but I've never heard anyone say that about him." He took another drag on his cigarette. "I know you're trying to find dirt on him. I don't know why, and I don't care. But from what I know of him, there isn't anything. Unless being a jackass qualifies."

"That's all right," I said. "You've helped me get a sense of the man." And left me curious about what had made him so angry.

"Sorry to disappoint you." He finished his cigarette and tossed the butt onto the ground.

"I'm used to it," I said.

"I've got to get back." He started to roll up his window, then said, "I'd be careful about dealing with Colonel Cooper. He's got friends in high places."

"I'll keep that in mind." I casually nodded at him.

He pulled slowly away from my car and turned onto

Quebec. I tapped the steering wheel as he drove away. Colonel Cooper had received a call that made him mad, but it was a good guess that Ray had misunderstood who it was from. It wasn't 'Buster,' but 'Lester.' Colonel Cooper had denied blackmailing Edith, or knowing Lester. It appeared he was lying, but just how deeply was he involved? I didn't know, but it was time to find out.

CHAPTER TWENTY-FIVE

I stopped at the White Spot for a quick lunch, and it only took me five minutes to get from there to Fred Cooper's house. Smoke swirled up from the chimney, so I assumed someone was home. I parked the Plymouth right in front of his house and marched up the sidewalk to the front porch. I knocked on the door and waited. From inside, a man yelled, a kid laughed, and then the door swung open. Colonel Cooper had his back to me.

"...get this and then we'll finish that game," he was saying.

He turned and saw me. He hadn't shaved today and a stubble of beard accentuated sudden lines of horror on his face. His mouth dropped open but no words came out.

"I need a word with you," I said, enjoying his predicament.

"What are you doing here?" he finally managed to say.

"We need to talk."

He shook his head emphatically. "I can't!" he hissed.

I planted my feet firmly on the ground. "I'm not going anywhere."

"Fred? Who is it?" a high, feminine voice asked.

The woman I'd seen the other day appeared behind him.

She pulled a red sweater tight around her tan dress to ward off the frigid air blasting through the door. She peered past him at me. I glanced at her, then back to Cooper. His eyes pleaded with me not to divulge his secret.

"This is Dewey Webb," he finally said. "He's with the, uh, Veterans Bureau. We talked the other day about a matter concerning a vet who served with me during the war. I didn't tell you that?"

"Smooth," I murmured.

He glared at me.

"No, you didn't." She gestured at the door. "You're letting in the cold, so why don't you ask him in."

He reluctantly held the door open and I entered into a decent-sized living room.

"I'm sorry to bother you at home," I said to Cooper, "but it's an urgent matter."

He turned to his wife. "Uh, could you give us a minute in private?"

"Of course." She looked at me. "Would you like a cup of coffee?" she asked.

"Thank you, ma'am, but no," I said as I took off my hat.

"Have a seat." She waved at a new yellow couch that sat under the front window.

I moved over and sat down, but Cooper remained standing. She smiled at me curiously before going to the kitchen. Through the doorway, I could see their two kids sitting at a table with a Monopoly board game between them.

"Let's go down into the basement," she said to them. "Your father has some business to take care of."

"Aw, Mom," the boy said.

"Take the game," she said.

They picked up the pieces and board, and threw it into a box. Chairs screeched on the floor, a door creaked open and footsteps pounded wooden stairs. The door shut and it was silent.

Cooper turned to me. "I ought to…"

"Keep your trap shut," I said.

He stalked over to an easy chair that sat across from the couch and perched on the edge of it. The fire in the corner fireplace had died to orange embers, but it heated the room nicely.

"What's the idea of coming here?" he demanded.

"You're lying to me." I pointed to the kitchen. "It seems you're good at it. Telling your wife I was with the Veterans Bureau – smooth."

"I am not lying!"

"You know Lester Klassen, and he knows you."

"That's not true!"

"He's been calling you, hasn't he?"

"How do you know that?" He realized his mistake and said, "I haven't heard a word from him."

I leaned forward. "If you don't tell me what's going on," I growled, "I'm going to tell your wife everything."

"You wouldn't," he said without conviction.

"Try me."

He glanced back toward the kitchen, making sure that she wasn't listening. He gnawed at a fingernail and sucked in a shaky breath. "Lester called me about a week ago. He told me who he was and said he wanted to talk to me. I put him off for a day, and then he waited outside the house, just like you did, only he was on foot. Our conversation was short. He told me that he knew about the affair and pregnancy, and he wanted a thousand dollars. He said if I didn't pay, he'd tell my wife. But he smelled like booze and could barely stand up, and he looked like he hadn't taken a bath in a week, so I thought he was bluffing. And even if he did say something to my wife, I thought I could dismiss his story as the ramblings of an old drunk. I told him to get lost and I wasn't too nice about it." He covered a fist with the palm of his other hand to emphasize the threat he'd made. "He left."

"But he kept badgering you."

He nodded. "I was livid, but I wasn't sure what to do. I finally told him that I'd come up with the money, but I needed more time. And then you showed up asking questions."

I hadn't seen this coming. Lester had been trying to black-mail both Edith and Cooper?

"Why didn't you tell me this yesterday?" I asked.

"You surprised me and I wasn't thinking clearly. All I want is for this to go away. Since I talked to you, I thought maybe you'd get after Lester and I wouldn't have to do anything." He sighed. "After all this time, I don't want to get involved in this."

I stared at him. He had no feelings for Edith, but was concerned only for himself.

"You *are* involved," I said. "You had a baby with Edith."

"No one needs to know that," he whispered.

"Had you met Lester before this?"

"No, but Edith talked about him. She said he was nothing but a no-good drunk, and that if her sister were smart, she'd leave him."

"When did you last hear from him?"

"The day before yesterday, in the morning. He called me at the base. He'd phoned the house first and made up some story about needing to get in touch with me right away, and my wife gave him the number. I was furious."

That confirmed what Sergeant Parise had told me. Whether Cooper had talked to Lester after the call to the base, I had no way of knowing. I was watching him carefully as he talked. For once, he didn't seem to be lying. He was too scared.

I changed the subject suddenly. "Tell me about the St. Gaudens."

"Who's that?" he asked. "Is that a saint or something? I'm not Catholic."

He seemed genuinely puzzled.

"It's nothing," I said. "Did Edith ever talk about her father?"

"Just that he'd passed away. I think she missed him."

"What about coins?"

"Coins?" He shook his head. "What does her father have to do with her being blackmailed?"

"Nothing," I repeated.

He shrugged, then stood up and tiptoed to the kitchen doorway. He glanced inside, listened for a second, and came back into the living room. He stared down at me, and for the first time, I saw a hint of remorse. "I know I've made some mistakes, but you need to tell Lester to leave me alone."

"Lester's dead."

He sank slowly back into the chair. "You're kidding. What happened?"

"Someone," I waited a long beat, "stabbed him. Now your problem's solved." He looked away. "What's your alibi for two nights ago, or maybe yesterday morning?"

He jerked a thumb at his chest. "You think *I* killed him?"

"If you did, then you don't have to pay him anything, and no one knows about your affair. You have a lot to lose if the wrong people find out."

"You're crazy. I never saw Lester after he came here. As for yesterday morning, I was at work, and last night, my wife and I were at the base for a party. But you can't ask people there about me."

"I'll talk to whoever I want."

His eyes grew hard. "I know people who can make things very uncomfortable for you."

"I've been threatened by worse," I said.

Just then, the basement door squeaked open. A moment

later, Cooper's wife poked her head into the living room. "I'm getting milk for the kids. Are you sure you're all right, Mr. Webb?"

Before I could answer, Cooper said, "Honey, I was just telling Mr. Webb about the party on the base last night."

She came into the living room and patted him lightly on the shoulder. "Where you promised we wouldn't stay too long, and then we were there half the night?" She shook her head at me. "I'm still tired."

He smiled triumphantly at me. "I tried to get away," he said to her, "but when Colonel Kelly gets going, you know what happens."

She gave me a pseudo-frown. "They like to sit around and tell war stories."

I nodded. "I understand."

Her comments came out too naturally for her to be lying.

"You're sure I can't get you anything?" she said to me.

I thought for a second. I'd gotten everything I was going to get out of Cooper. "That's very kind of you, but I need to be going."

Cooper stared anxiously at me, worried that I would reveal his secret.

"Yes, I think we're done here," he said to her.

"I see." She smiled politely.

I stood up. Cooper jumped to his feet and he and his wife walked me to the door.

"I hope you have a good afternoon," she said. "Stay warm."

"I will," I said.

I donned my hat, stepped outside, and glanced back at them. Cooper hurriedly closed the door. As I walked to my car, I turned back to the house. Cooper stood at the window, watching me. I was sure he wouldn't relax until I was long gone.

CHAPTER TWENTY-SIX

I spent the rest of the afternoon in a fruitless search for Sonny O'Hara and Boyd Schuler. I first stopped by Sonny's apartment building again, but he wasn't home. The landlady was in, but she hadn't seen him, either. I escaped her apartment before she was able to rope me into a long conversation. I waited outside in the Plymouth with the engine running, but then left before someone got suspicious. I next popped in and out of some of the bars on Larimer Street. As I walked around, I was quickly reminded I was not in a good part of town.

Larimer Street had been the original main street of Denver, staked out in 1858 by General William H. Larimer, Jr. But now it was a twenty-five block skid row, with small businesses, flophouses, cheap hotels, pawn shops for quick cash, missions for free meals, and plenty of cheap bars and pool halls. The buildings, once considered fancy, were now run-down with multiple layers of grime. It was a great area to find a day labor job to earn enough for an evening of drinking. This afternoon, however, the crowds were sparse, and I never saw Boyd Schuler, so I drove home.

Sam was down for a nap, so Clara and I had time to talk. Once Sam awoke, I played with him for a while and then had dinner. When I told Clara I had to work again, she was disappointed, but she didn't complain. Before I went to the bars on Larimer, I decided to stop at the office to see if anyone had disturbed it again, and to call Ruby Klassen.

The building was dark when I arrived, and when I checked the front door, it was locked. I let myself in and trotted upstairs to my office. The doorknob hadn't been fixed yet, and the outer door was still slightly ajar. I went inside and closed the door as best I could. No notes were on the floor, so I unlocked the inner door and crossed to the window. I stayed to the side of the window and peeked outside. The street was empty. I shut the blinds, sat down at my desk and turned on the lamp, then dialed Ruby Klassen.

"It's Dewey Webb," I said when she answered.

"Did you find out anything more?" she asked impatiently.

"I'm getting close." I swiveled in my chair and looked out the window into the darkness. "Does the name Boyd Schuler mean anything to you?"

"No. Should it?"

"I would've been surprised if you'd said yes."

"He's blackmailing Edith?"

"He's involved, but I still haven't found who's behind this."

"We've got to get to the bottom of this soon or I'm going to have to sell all of Dad's coins."

"I know. Do me a favor, and call Edith and fill her in."

"I will," she said. She thanked me and hung up.

I set the phone down, sat back in my chair, and lit a cigarette. I blew smoke into the air and mulled things over. I had a lot of disparate information, but nothing that led me to Edith's blackmailer. If I could find Sonny O'Hara or Boyd Schuler, would that clear things up? I checked my watch. It was a little early to head down to Larimer Street, so I kept thinking through the case and watched the minutes tick by.

A while later, a noise pulled me from my thoughts. I leaned forward and strained my ears to hear. I wasn't sure if it was my imagination, so I set my cigarette in the ashtray, stood up and went to the window. I gazed through the blinds and scrutinized the street carefully. No one was about. I looked out for another minute, and then I heard a sound again. It came from downstairs.

I slipped around the desk and into the waiting room. I strode softly to the door and listened. One of the old wooden stairs creaked, and then another. Someone was coming slowly upstairs. No tenant would sneak around the building, so who was it?

I took out my gun and checked through the crack in the door. I could see the top of the stairs. The hall was dark, just dim streetlight from the window at the end barely lighting the corridor. Then a shadowy figure materialized at the top of the stairs. The figure was dark but I could easily make out a pork pie hat. The figure turned and started tiptoeing down the hall toward me. In two strides I was across the office. I pulled my office door partway closed, so just a sliver of light fell into the waiting room. I moved back across the room and positioned myself to the side of the door. I raised the Colt, narrowed my eyes and waited.

A floorboard just outside the door creaked and I heard heavy breathing. Then the door slowly swung inward. A long moment passed, and the figure stepped into the waiting room. As he skulked toward my office, the light from the inner office illuminated his face. It was Sonny, in jeans and a leather coat that I'm sure he thought made him look tough. He held up a knife with a long, thin blade.

He took another step, and I swiftly stepped up behind him

and chopped down on his forearm with the butt of my gun. He yowled and dropped the knife. He started to turn around. I kicked the knife away and grabbed his arm with my free hand. He tried to get away and ran into the desk. Papers next to the typewriter fell to the floor. I yanked him backward. He stumbled, and I used a foot to swipe his legs out from under him. He landed with a thud on the couch and his hat fell to the floor. He cursed loudly and I slapped him across the face, then backhanded him.

"What the –" he said. Blood trickled from his nose, and he wiped it away.

I shoved the gun into his face. "Looking for me?"

His eyes grew wide and he sputtered excuses. I slapped him again.

"Take it easy!" he pleaded with me. He raised his hands in surrender.

"You're the one who showed up with a knife," I snarled. "Why shouldn't I pop a cap in you right now?"

He shook. "Please, I wasn't going to hurt you."

"Right," I said sarcastically. "Why'd you come here? Who sent you?"

"I'm on my own."

I slapped his cheek again with my free hand. Even in the dim light I could see a red mark.

"Hey!" he whined. "What'd you do that for?"

"You're a bad liar, Sonny." I shoved the gun into his forehead. "And I'm tired of the games."

"I was going to scare you, that's all!"

"You were going to do more than that," I said. "Who sent you?"

"All right!" His hands trembled. "Get that gun out of my face and I'll tell you."

I glared at him. "You try anything, I'll shoot you."

"I won't!"

I stood up and stared at him.

He rubbed his forearm. "I think you broke my wrist."

"Right now you're alive, but you better start talking."

He shifted on the couch and groaned. "It was Boyd."

"Boyd Schuler."

"Yeah, he said I needed to take care of you."

"So you decided to break in while I was here, and you didn't think I'd hear you?"

"Boyd said the downstairs door would be open, but it wasn't, so I had to jimmy the lock."

That had been the noise I'd heard. And Boyd must've been the one who'd broken into my office before, and he'd found the downstairs door open because another tenant had forgotten to lock it.

"Why does Boyd want me out of the way?" I asked.

"I don't know." I raised my hand to smack him again. "I don't!" he yelled. "He said if I wanted the big money he'd been promising, I had to get rid of you."

"Did you get rid of Lester Klassen?"

He shook his head. "Boyd did that, I swear." His eyes darted all around. "And he said it was on me to take care of you."

"Why'd Boyd kill Lester?"

"He didn't tell me."

"How much do you know about Edith Sandalwood?"

"Who?"

"The dame you're blackmailing."

He was bewildered. "I didn't know her name."

I aimed the gun at him.

"I didn't know her!" he said. "It's the truth!"

"How'd you get involved in this?"

183

"Boyd talked to me one night at a bar. He asked me if I wanted to make an easy fifty bucks. I said why not, and he told me he had someone who wanted money from a woman he knew, and this guy wanted to hire us to get it from her. My job was to meet this doll and she would give me some money. Once I got it, I'd meet up with him later and I'd get my cut and he'd take the rest to this other guy."

"Why didn't you take the money and run?"

He snorted. "You don't double-cross Boyd unless you want an early grave."

"Why didn't Boyd go himself?"

"He was following the doll – Edith – to see where she went."

"Why'd he care about that?"

"He didn't tell me."

"The first time you met the woman, she didn't have all the money."

"Yeah, Boyd said she probably wouldn't, and told me to tell her we'd give her more time. But when I met her the second time, the plan had changed, and Boyd said to ask her for more money. So I got the money she had and said she needed to get more."

"And that's all you know?"

"Yeah."

"You're the middleman only. Boyd's been giving you instructions, and you follow them without asking questions."

He nodded. "I don't care what it's about, as long as the dough's good."

"How much are you being paid to knock me off?"

"Boyd said if we don't get rid of you, we don't get any dough at all."

"How much is your cut?" I said forcefully.

"A few hundred at least, maybe a lot more, if we get the dough from that woman."

"I didn't know my death would come so cheap."

He laughed, then choked it off when I slapped him again.

"Ow!" He rubbed his jaw.

"Who hired you and Boyd?"

"I don't know. Don't hit me again, because that's the truth."

I wasn't surprised. He didn't even know who Edith was, so how likely was it that he knew who had planned the whole thing.

"Where's Boyd now?" I asked.

He shrugged. "He likes Joe's Buffet, or The Royal. They're about a block apart. He'll probably be at one of them tonight."

I stared down at him. He was rubbing his arm again, and he looked like a scolded dog, small and quivering for mercy. And he was scared – that he'd been caught, and scared of Boyd. Chet's assessment of Sonny fit. He wasn't the brains of the operation, and he wasn't nearly the tough guy he thought he was. I took a step back and kicked his leg.

"You listening to me?"

He nodded.

"I'm going to let you go, but if I ever see you around again, I'll take that shot at you. I saw guys a lot more dangerous than you during the war, and I easily took them out. Don't think I won't do the same with you."

He turned pale. For all his bravado, he was smart enough not to say anything.

"Now beat it," I growled.

He shoved himself off the couch, swiped his hat off the floor, and jammed it on his head. Then he bolted out the door. I went into the hall and heard footsteps on the stairs. Then the front door opened and slammed shut. I hurried over to the hall window and looked out. Sonny was running down the street. I rubbed my hand. I might've been harder on him than I needed to be, but I'd gotten information from him.

I holstered the Colt and walked slowly back into my office. I retrieved Sonny's knife and dropped it into a desk drawer. Then I straightened up the waiting room, pulled the door closed, and left for Larimer Street.

CHAPTER TWENTY-SEVEN

I arrived in lower downtown a few minutes after eight o'clock. I parked two blocks down from Joe's Buffet, one of the bars Boyd Schuler frequented. I locked the Plymouth and strode down Larimer, keeping my eye out for Boyd. Blue-collar workers, farm laborers who came into town for the weekend, and women looking for a good time crowded the street. A salty smell, like stale sweat, permeated the chilly night air. I jostled my way past a popular bar, then heard a whistle and a shout. I looked up. A woman in a worn red dress that showed a generous amount of cleavage was hanging out a second story window. Her face was heavily painted with makeup and she clutched a bottle of dark liquid in her hand.

"Hey, hon, you're a looker," she called down to me. "How about buyin' me a drink?"

"Looks like you already have one," I said, then shook my head and moved on.

I pulled my hat down low. I felt too obvious here, a little too clean-cut. I passed the Zaza Theater and came upon a bar with a huge front window. 'Joe's Buffet' was painted in large gold letters across it. Two men in old suits loitered near the door, smoking cigarettes. After my encounter with Sonny O'Hara, I was ready for trouble, but they moved away, and I was able to go inside without issue.

The joint was packed. Thick smoke hung in the air, along with a stench of cheap booze. The heavy twang of country music bounced off the walls, and loud voices shouted above the music. I sidled up to the bar and squeezed into a small spot. I ordered a Scotch, gulped it down, then turned and slowly surveyed the place.

People stood two and three deep near the bar. Others crammed themselves into small booths. A few couples danced in tiny pockets of free space between the bar and the booths. Alcohol flowed generously. I didn't see Boyd, so I moseyed down the bar and glanced into the booths. Everyone was drinking too much to pay me any mind. At the far end of the bar was a door. I opened it to find a short hallway. At the end of it, an old oak wall telephone hung on the wall. To the right, through another open door, I saw a toilet and sink.

A man jostled past me and toward the bathroom. I pulled the hall door closed and snaked back toward the front of the bar. I rechecked the booths on my way to the door. Still no Boyd. I reached the front of the bar and stopped short. Boyd Schuler and Sonny O'Hara were standing outside the window. I ducked behind a dancing couple and squeezed into a space at the bar, then glanced toward the window.

Sonny was saying something, and it was obvious he was in a panic, his eyes wide, his hands raised, pleading his case. Boyd jabbed a finger in Sonny's face and Sonny backed up. Sonny was ratting me out. And he was panicking. The dialogue continued, and then Boyd suddenly slapped Sonny across the face. Sonny backed up and gingerly touched his cheek. After the beating I'd given him, and now a blow from Boyd, his jaw must've been hurting bad. He backpedaled, yelled something at Boyd, and then sprinted off.

Boyd shook his head and then stormed into the bar. I turned sideways and pulled my hat down to shield my face, but I didn't need to worry about Boyd seeing me, because he strode past the throngs of people to the back of the bar without looking at anyone. He reached the hallway door, opened it and vanished. I dashed after him and reached the door as it was swinging closed. I pushed it open. Boyd was at the phone, his back to me.

I slipped into the hall just as the man I'd seen before came out of the bathroom. I used him as a shield and sprang into the bathroom. A sour reek hit me, and I coughed and put a hand to my nose to keep from gagging. Then I cracked the door and listened. The hall door had closed and the music and voices diminished to a lower din. Boyd began talking and I strained to hear him.

"...talked to Sonny," he was saying. "No, he didn't take care of him...Sonny went to his office, but the guy pulled a fast one on him, and he got away. Sonny doesn't know where he is."

Sonny had lied to Boyd, and didn't tell Boyd what I'd done to him.

"Yeah, I know that detective might foul everything up," Boyd said. "What can I say? I thought Sonny could handle it, but don't worry, he's still looking for the guy now...I told you, we'll find him, but you're paying big for this." Another pause, and then Boyd's voice grew intense. "I *know*. Listen, I never wanted to kill anyone, okay? But I took care of Lester, and we'll take care of the detective, so you better come through on *your* end. We want big money for this."

The hall door opened and Hank Williams blared loudly into the tiny hallway. A short, stocky man tried to push open the bathroom door. I held it closed, but he cursed and shoved harder. I stepped back suddenly and he lurched forward. I grabbed him before he hit the floor and lifted him up.

"It's occupied, got it?" I snarled.

"Uh, yeah, okay," he said.

My eyes burned from his alcohol breath. I let go and he stumbled back into the hall. He grumbled something, but I'd already cracked the bathroom door again. The music faded and I heard Boyd talking, but I'd missed something.

"Yeah, Cecil, we're on track. Sonny will be there to get the money from the dame. But you've gotta pay us first...No, I want our cut now...I know it's not what we agreed, but things have gotten out of hand...You can handle this on your own, if you want...I thought that's what you would say. Fine. I'll be over to get it and then we'll talk about next time."

Boyd slammed the receiver back onto the hook and a second later, he passed by the bathroom. Hank Williams grew louder as the hall door opened. I waited until it started to close and then I stepped out of the bathroom. As I went back into the bar, the stocky guy tried to stop me.

"I just wanted to −" he started to say but I pushed him aside.

Boyd was almost to the front door. I elbowed my way through the crowd and out the door. Boyd had paused by the bar next door. I stepped over to a lamppost, leaned against it, and glanced in his direction. He had pulled paper and a bag of tobacco out of his pocket. He took a moment to roll a cigarette, then lit it and took a puff as he watched a woman in a tight skirt saunter past. Then he hurried up the street and I followed. After three blocks, he turned the corner. I dodged past people to catch up, paused by a cheap hotel, and peeked around the side of the building. Boyd had stopped by a dark-colored Mercury with a bent front fender. I'd seen that car at the Rexall. Sonny said that Boyd had been following Edith, and I'd seen him that day.

I continued to watch Boyd. Without a worry that anyone might see, he pulled out a pistol, checked it, then got in the Mercury. The engine revved to life, headlights burst into the darkness, and the car squealed off down the street.

I watched it go, then started back for my car. As I walked back along Larimer Street, I thought about the conversation I'd overheard. Boyd had said that Sonny was still searching for me. I allowed myself a small smile. Sonny was in such a panic he lied to Boyd about what had happened at my office. And if Sonny was smart, he lied about looking for me now. But I'd keep alert anyway, in case he was lurking about.

And Boyd had admitted to killing Lester. I wondered if he'd stabbed Lester in order to make it appear that Sonny had done it, knowing that Sonny's weapon of choice was a knife. But why had Boyd knocked off Lester? What had Lester been doing that Boyd wanted him out of the way?

Then something else occurred to me. Boyd had rolled his own cigarette. Just like the guy who'd been spying outside my office the other night, and like whoever'd been at Sonny's house waiting for him to come home. Boyd got around. But who was paying them to do all this?

I suddenly stopped. A man bumped into me, cursed and moved on, but I barely noticed. I realized what I'd been missing. Boyd had mentioned the name 'Cecil.' I'd heard that name before. A customer had used it when he talked to the guy at Denver Stamp and Coin. Pieces started falling into place. Norman Dewitt, the drunk at the bar near Lester's apartment, had seen a tall, clean-cut man visiting Lester. I'd assumed it was Fred Cooper, but what if it had been Cecil? What if he'd devised a plan with Lester to blackmail Edith? And Sonny O'Hara's landlady had overheard Sonny and Boyd talking about how much something was worth. Were they talking about Cecil and the coins? Who better to know about a coin collection and its value than the owner of a coin shop?

I went over my conversations with Cecil, and something else clicked into place. The first time I'd talked to him, he'd said that John Norland only owned one St. Gaudens, but the next time, he'd told me that Norland had a bunch of them. Why change his story? I shook my head. It certainly looked like Cecil was involved. And I'd played right into his hands by giving him my card, so he knew right where to send someone – Sonny – to get rid of me.

An idea popped into my head and I ran back to Joe's Buffet. I went straight back to the wooden wall phone and called Edith Sandalwood. Gordon answered, so I hung up, waited a minute and called back. This time Edith answered.

"It's Dewey Webb."

"Yes, I remembered your signal." She was whispering. "I'm in the bedroom."

"I'll make it fast," I said. "Can you recall your conversation with the owner of Denver Stamp and Coin?"

"I didn't say much to him," she said.

"Did you tell him why you were selling the coin?"

"No. He asked where I'd gotten the coin, so I told him about Dad, but that was it. I didn't say why I needed the money and he didn't ask. Why?"

"I'll explain later," I said. "You better hang up before Gordon gets suspicious. Tell him it was a wrong number." I hoped she'd be able to pull that off.

I hung up and stared at the wall. Cecil had told me Edith needed the money to pay someone back. Had I made him nervous enough so that he started lying to cover for himself? Only one way to find out. I left the bar, and started running back down Larimer, past the Zaza Theater, to my car. It was time to pay Cecil a visit. If I could find any evidence to prove that he was blackmailing Edith, or get him to trip up and tell me how he was involved, then I'd have something to take to the police. The problem was, I didn't know Cecil's last name or where he lived. And I would have to play a game of cat-and-mouse with Boyd. Could I get to Cecil before Boyd got to me?

CHAPTER TWENTY-EIGHT

I was glad to leave Larimer Street and its cacophony of people and noise behind. I weaved through downtown to Broadway and took it south to Denver Stamp and Coin. I parked across the street and watched the store for a moment. It was completely dark. I doubted Cecil was there, but if I could somehow get inside, I could check his paperwork and see if I could find his home address. Traffic was sparse, so I waited until there were no cars nearby, then I ran across Broadway to the store. I peered in the front window, then tried the door. Locked, as I would've expected, with a bolt that I knew I couldn't break.

I heard a car coming down Broadway, so I started walking casually down the street. I waited until it passed, then ducked around the side of the building. I checked the store windows, but none opened. I looked in them, but didn't see any lights on or movement. I made my way around to the back and found the rear door, but this too was secure. I spotted a trashcan near the door and rummaged around in it, holding papers up and reading them by moonlight, but I didn't find anything that would tell me Cecil's last name. I finally gave up. I wiped my hands on my slacks and glanced up at the moon. It was bright and full. I checked my watch. Almost ten o'clock. I wondered if Edith or Ruby would know more about Cecil. If I called Edith again tonight, Gordon might get suspicious. But I could talk to Ruby, even though it was late.

I dashed back to the Plymouth and drove up Broadway until I spotted a gas station with a pay phone. I parked and called Ruby.

She answered with a hesitant hello.

"It's Dewey Webb," I said.

"Why are you calling so late? Is something wrong?"

"Sorry, but it's important. Did your father ever talk about the owner of Denver Stamp and Coin?"

"Hmm," she said. "Nothing in particular, just that he visited the shop or he bought a coin, something like that."

"I know you said the coins are in a safety deposit box, but do you have any of your father's paperwork?"

"Yes, I've got two or three boxes around here. Why?"

"I need to find out the shop owner's full name, and it's possible your father kept some paperwork related to the coins he bought and sold."

"Is the shop owner the one blackmailing Edith?"

"That's what I intend to find out."

"Come on over. I'll dig out the boxes for when you get here."

"Thanks."

I hung up and made a beeline to Ruby's house. She opened the door as I was coming up the walk.

"I found three boxes," she said as she held the door open for me, "but I haven't found any paperwork from the shop."

I came inside and followed her into the kitchen, where she

had three large apple boxes on the table. One was open and papers were stacked on the table.

She gestured at the other boxes. "Help yourself."

I tossed my hat on a chair and started rifling through a box. "Would Edith know the shop owner's name?" I asked.

She shook her head. "I already called her and asked, but she didn't know."

I flipped through papers. "Here are some receipts," I said after a while, "but nothing with any information on Cecil."

"I can understand that Cecil would know how much Dad's collection might be worth, but how did he know about Edith?" Ruby asked as she dug through a box.

"I don't know if Lester talked to him, or if Boyd talked to someone in Limon or Vernon who knew about the affair."

"Who's Boyd?"

"Boyd Schuler. He's been doing Cecil's dirty work, along with Sonny O'Hara."

Her brow wrinkled, and I explained what I'd learned.

"Unbelievable," she said.

I nodded. I finished with the box I had and dug into the third box. I took out some papers and then found a small blue book.

"What's this?"

Ruby stared at it and shrugged. I flipped the book open.

"It's notations on coins," I said. I turned pages and scanned the notes. I was about to give up and toss the book aside when I noticed some initials: DSC.

"DSC," I muttered.

Ruby had been looking over my shoulder. "Denver Stamp and Coin?"

"Makes sense to me."

We read through more notes and then Ruby suddenly pointed at a page. "There!"

197

She was right. Underneath a note about a coin from 1898 was "Cecil Tipton will look for it."

"Tipton. That's his last name," Ruby said.

I set the book down. "Where's your phone directory?"

She dug it out of a cabinet drawer and handed it to me. I thumbed through it until I found the T's, and then I found a listing for Cecil A.

"He lives east of downtown," she said.

I handed the phone book back to her. "I'm glad you didn't get rid of this paperwork."

She smiled. "Me, too."

I retrieved my hat and she followed me to the front door.

"Do you want me to call the police?" she asked.

I shook my head. "I can't prove anything yet. But when I do, I'll call them."

"How are you going to prove it?"

"I'm going to beat a confession out of him," I said.

She was taken aback, not sure if she should believe me. "Be careful," she finally said.

I pushed my hat down low and headed out the door.

———

Cecil Tipton lived in a modest brick house on Clarkson Street, a stone's throw from downtown. I parked a block away and walked back down the street. It was quiet, too cold for anyone to be out and about. I didn't even hear a dog. I stooped down by a hedge that separated Cecil's yard from his neighbor's, then studied Cecil's house. A light was on in the front window, but the shade was drawn. A side window was dark. Was he home? I wasn't beyond breaking and entering in order to find evidence of his blackmailing Edith. Before I could make a decision, head-lights appeared at the end of the street. I ducked down behind the hedge and waited. Boyd's Mercury soon approached. He parked right in front of Cecil's house, cut the engine, hopped out and strode up the steps to the front porch. He banged on the door and it opened almost immediately. Cecil Tipton was a silhouette against bright light.

"I thought you were coming right over," Cecil said in a low voice.

"I stopped by my apartment first," Boyd said.

"You shouldn't be coming here."

Boyd shrugged. "I want my money now."

"And I want you to take care of that detective, not Sonny."

"I will. You pay me first, and then I'll go by his house tonight and get rid of him."

"What if he's not there?"

"I've watched his house a time or two. He's got a wife. I'll make her tell me where he is. Look, you don't have to worry about it, but you gotta pay me first."

Cecil shook his head in disgust. "Get in here." He stepped aside and Boyd walked in. The door quietly shut.

Fear coursed through me, not for myself, but for Clara and Sam. I couldn't risk having Boyd come to my house. I had to put an end to this now. But if I called the police, it would be my word against theirs. I'd have to handle this on my own.

I stole to the end of the hedge and into Cecil's yard. I rushed up to the house and tried to peek into the front window, but I couldn't see anything. I hurried around the side of the house. Another window was lit yellow, so I sneaked up to it and looked inside. Boyd was sitting on a couch, and Cecil was pacing the room. Across from the couch were two wingback chairs, and a desk sat against the wall by the doorway.

I made my way past two tin trashcans toward the back of the house. The yard was tiny, with a walk that led to a dark alley. There was no fence, so I slipped up onto a small back porch. I tried the back door, but it was locked. It was a heavy door, and I didn't think I could break it down. And I wanted the element of surprise. I looked around and an idea formed. I stepped off the porch and back around the side of the house. I paused by the trashcans, then banged on one of them. The sound clattered into the dark night. I didn't have to wait long before the back door opened and a rectangle of light fell into the backyard.

"Go see what it is," Cecil said.

"Why don't you go?" Boyd asked.

"Are you scared?" Cecil's mocking tone hit right at Boyd, questioning his manhood. "After all, you have a knife and a gun."

"All right," Boyd snapped. He wasn't thrilled about going out into the darkness.

Footsteps clomped on the wood steps. I pressed my back to the side of the house and waited. A shadow soon appeared at the corner. Boyd had drawn his gun, and he was tiptoeing toward the neighbor's house. When he reached me, I grabbed his arm and yanked him toward me.

"What –" he started to say.

In one swift move, I knocked the gun out of his hand, flipped his arm up behind his back, and slammed him into the side of the house. His breath came out in a gasp, then I clamped my free hand over his mouth. He struggled, and I pushed up on his arm, straining the shoulder socket. He grunted.

"Boyd, where are you?" Cecil called out. "What's going on?"

"Tell him it's nothing," I whispered in Boyd's ear. "Do it, or I'll break your arm!"

Boyd made another muffled sound, but he quit struggling. I uncovered his mouth.

"I'm fine," Boyd said loudly. His voice shook. "It's nothing."

"Is someone out there?" Cecil asked.

I forced his arm up farther and he groaned again.

"Tell him no," I muttered.

"No," Boyd gasped loudly.

"Tell him you're going to check around and then you'll come back inside," I whispered.

"I, uh..." he hesitated.

I shoved him into the wall and his head banged against the siding.

"What was that noise?" Cecil asked.

"Uh, I tripped," Boyd said.

"Good," I whispered. "Now tell him you're looking around." He didn't say anything. "Do it!" I hissed.

"I'll look around and then come back inside," Boyd repeated my words.

"Fine, but don't take too long," Cecil said.

The back door partially closed and the rectangle of light morphed into a sliver.

"We'll get you for this," Boyd snarled.

"You've got me quaking in my boots," I said. I put my hand on his shoulder and stepped back, and unholstered my gun. Then I wrenched his arm behind his back again.

"Hey!" he said.

"Shut up and move." I gripped his arm with one hand and wrapped my other arm around his neck, my gun resting against his cheek. "You see this gun?"

He nodded.

"Try anything and you'll be dead. Now start walking."

I guided him around the back of the house and up the porch steps. When we reached the back door, I kicked it open with my foot and propelled him into the kitchen.

"Don't try anything funny," I murmured.

I pushed him past the table and down the hallway. When we

reached the living room, I shoved him, and as I did so, I kicked his legs out from under him. He tripped and fell to the floor.

"Boyd, what's going –" Cecil turned around and saw me, but he kept his cool.

I pointed the Colt at him. "Don't move."

Cecil slowly raised his hands. "Please don't do anything rash, Mr. Webb."

"We'll see about that," I said.

CHAPTER TWENTY-NINE

Boyd rolled over and got to his knees.

"Stay there," I ordered him.

He glared up at me and leaned against the couch, but kept quiet. Like Sonny, he wasn't as tough as he thought he was.

"Is there something I can help you with?" Cecil asked. His smooth, cultured voice grated on my ears. And his neatly pressed slacks and white shirt, and his green sweater irritated me, too. He looked anything but a crook, and that's what had me wary.

"Don't play dumb," I said. "I know you're blackmailing Edith Sandalwood."

He gazed at me, his expression neutral. "And how did you come to this conclusion?"

I pointed at Boyd with the gun. "He and his pal Sonny O'Hara led me to you."

Boyd's face flushed red, and he grunted something unintelligible.

Cecil frowned at Boyd, disappointment on his face. "Really?"

"And I overheard you and Boyd talking about getting rid of me," I said. "Sonny tried, but here I am."

Cecil turned back to me. He blinked a few times, then sighed. He seemed resigned to the situation. "Yes, it's unfortunate Sonny couldn't be relied upon. Or Boyd. It seems I'll have to take care of things myself."

"That's too bad," I said dryly.

He gestured at the chair. "May I? I don't like to stand for long."

"Yeah." I narrowed my eyes at him, still wary. "Don't try anything funny."

"Thank you, and I won't." He eased down into the chair, took off his glasses, and put them in a sweater pocket. "I have a bad back. Compliments of the first World War."

"If you hope to gain my sympathies, it won't work," I said.

He emitted a short laugh. "I'm sure you're right." A small smile crossed his face. "You have caught me, as they say. And I deserve whatever comes to me."

He was playing me, but I wasn't sure how. What did he hope to gain by being so cooperative?

"I've got most of this figured out," I said, mimicking his casual tone in the hopes that he'd keep talking. "Why not just buy the coins from Edith and Ruby?"

"I did approach Ruby about it, but she didn't want to sell them."

"So you resorted to," I pointed at Boyd, "this whole scheme."

He let out a small breath.

"I don't understand why you waited until now," I said. "John Norland died a long time ago. Why not steal the coins then?"

He straightened his pant leg. "I am not, by trade, a thief. I never even considered resorting to criminal endeavors until my business took a turn for the worse. Then a fortunate turn of

fate occurred when Lester Klassen walked through the door. He
had a valuable coin he wanted to sell. It happened to be a coin
that I remember selling to John Norland. It was odd that
someone like Lester would own such a coin. He was not what
you'd picture as a numismatist. I asked Lester how it had come
into his possession. At first, he tried to lie about it, but, as I'm
sure you know, liquor loosens lips, and Lester had imbibed some
before he came into my store. I pressed him about the owner-
ship of the coin, and he eventually told me he'd stolen it from
his wife. It took a little coercing, but I found out that he had
been married to John's daughter."

"Ruby," I said.

"Yes," he nodded thoughtfully. "I realized that if Lester was
capable of stealing the coins, I could, too."

"So you broke into Ruby's house."

"You certainly have put the pieces together," he said.

"Why are you telling him all this?" Boyd snarled. "You
should keep your mouth shut."

Cecil crossed one leg over the other. "Oh, I don't mind," he
said. "You see Boyd, he's not going to leave here alive."

Boyd and I both glanced around warily. What was Cecil
planning? I needed to keep him talking until I could decipher
that.

"And when the coins weren't at Ruby's, you decided to
blackmail her," I said.

Boyd started to protest, but Cecil shushed him. Then he
turned back to me.

"Not finding the coins at Ruby's was disappointing," he said.
"I had Lester's number, so I called him and arranged a meeting.
I asked him if he knew where the collection was now, and he
said that he'd gotten into a fight with Ruby about the coins.
She'd told him that she had put them in a safety deposit box. It
seemed that this would end my foray into crime right then, and

that would be for the best, because I was not a very good thief. In fact, I was terrified when I broke into Ruby's house. But Lester, as always, was running his mouth about how he knew things about Ruby and Edith. I pushed him to tell me what, and after a bit of persuasion, he told me about Edith's pregnancy. He said that we could blackmail her, and she'd have to sell the coins to me in order to pay us and we could split the money. What he said actually made sense to me, so I agreed. Lester brought in Boyd and Sonny to deliver the notes to Edith and to meet her and get the money."

"How could you be so sure Edith would bring the coins to you to sell?" I asked.

"It was a risk, but I'm one of the few coin shops in town, and I surmised that if their father spoke about my shop, it would be the logical place that they would come to. And I'd spoken to Ruby about the coins, so I figured she would come to me first."

"You were right," I said. "And then, when Edith sold the coin to you, you got your money back, and you have the coin in your possession to sell."

He nodded. "Yes. I'm going to make a lot of money on Norland's coins."

"But working with a drunk like Lester wasn't very smart," I said.

"Yes, I wasn't thrilled about having him as a partner, but he took care of collecting the money from Edith, which was better for me. As I said, I do not have the penchant to be a good criminal, and I couldn't very well show up to collect the money myself." He fiddled with his pant leg again. "But then Lester got greedy and decided he wanted to keep all the money for himself."

"So you had Boyd kill him," I said.

"It was an accident," Boyd blurted. "I was just trying to

scare Lester and he went berserk. If I didn't kill him, he was going to kill me."

I had no way of knowing if Boyd was telling the truth, or if he was setting up his defense for later, but I'd let the police work that out.

"Yes, that's what he told me," Cecil agreed.

"What about blackmailing Fred Cooper?" I asked.

Cecil raised his eyebrows. "Who's Fred Cooper?"

"You don't know?"

He shook his head. "Should I?"

"He's the guy who got Edith pregnant. Lester was blackmailing him, too."

Cecil's brown eyes registered a tinge of respect. "Lester was working all the angles, wasn't he?"

"It looks that way," I said. "But why didn't you ask for the money all at once?"

"I didn't know if Edith would ask her sister for the coins. But once she did, I knew we should try for more money."

"Ruby said she wouldn't give any more of the coins to Edith."

"That thought had occurred to me. With a little persuasion, she could've been made to change her mind." He said it so coolly, it was disturbing. "It all seemed to be going according to plan." He tapped a hand on his knee. "Until you showed up."

"And then you had to take care of me," I said.

"Yes."

"You were so helpful when I came by the store, but you tried to throw me off track by telling me about the guy with gray hair," I said. "He doesn't exist, does he?"

"I see it didn't work very well," Cecil said.

"And you knew all along that John Norland had a valuable coin collection."

"Yes. Right before he passed away, John told me a lot more

about his collection, and the St. Gaudens. I knew that I could sell his coins for thousands of dollars. I have buyers lined up to take the coins off my hands."

"Why'd you send Boyd out to Limon?" I asked.

A faint look of surprise crossed his face and then was gone. "You know about that, too?" I nodded. "When John and I talked," he continued, "I told him he should be careful with his collection because of its value, and he said not to worry, that he had it well hidden on his property. When I decided to try to get the coins, I thought it would be worth seeing if anything was out at the property."

"And was there?"

He shrugged. "I don't know. I sent him out there," he nodded at Boyd on the floor, "but he wasn't able to get past the new owners to find out."

I'd have to check with Ruby to see if she knew anything about hidden coins.

"Well." He put his hands in his sweater pockets. "I think that's about it."

"What are you going to do now?" Boyd muttered from his place on the floor.

I glanced over at him. "Call the police. They'll be very interested in what you told me."

"I'm afraid I can't allow that," Cecil said.

"You think so?" I said.

He smiled that confident smile. "Yes."

And then I realized what he was up to. He didn't intend to go to jail. That was his plan from the moment I forced my way into the room. One of us would die. I saw that register in his eyes the second before he vaulted himself out of the chair at me, a small gun in his hand. I had no time but to do one thing: I pulled the trigger.

CHAPTER THIRTY

The bullet hit Cecil on the left shoulder. The impact spun him around and he landed back on the chair, then slumped to the floor. He put a hand over the wound. Blood seeped between his fingers, but he didn't utter a sound. His gun fell to the floor near Boyd. Boyd dove for it and grabbed it, but I stomped on his hand. He howled and loosened his grip. I kicked the gun and it skittered across the floor to the other side of the room. Then I noticed a hole in the wall behind me. Cecil had shot at me, but missed.

"Now, sit up slowly," I ordered Boyd.

He groaned. "I think you broke my fingers."

"I'll do more if you don't move."

Boyd growled obscenities at me, but he pushed himself back until he was again leaning against the couch. He cradled his hand in his lap and moaned.

Cecil remained by the chair. He stared up at me in defeat. "You should've killed me."

"Maybe," I said. "Where's the phone?"

"It's in the kitchen," Cecil said. He was turning pale as the pain set in.

"Thanks," I said, with no gratitude.

I backed up, but kept my eyes on both of them. I reached the kitchen doorway and found the phone on the wall. Then I called the police.

———

Once the police arrived, I spent the better part of the night explaining what had happened. Cecil didn't acknowledge or deny what he'd done, so for the moment, it was indeed my word against his. Boyd was not talking either, but I figured at some point, he or Sonny would worry about going to prison, and they might start singing. And then Cecil might cave in and admit to what he'd done.

The police asked me a lot of questions about firing my gun, and there would be an ongoing investigation, but I was confident I would be cleared of any charges. At dawn, I was allowed to leave. There was little traffic, and I was home in minutes. I sneaked into the house and checked on Clara.

"Is everything all right?" she asked, sitting up in bed.

"Yes," I said. "I'm sorry I woke you. Go back to sleep."

She shook her head as she got up and put on her robe. "I'm awake now. I'll check on Sam and then start breakfast."

"Thanks."

I went into the kitchen, and even though it was early, I called Ruby. She answered with fog in her voice.

"It's Dewey," I said.

She was instantly alert. "What happened? Did you talk to Cecil Tipton? Was he involved?"

"Yes," I said. "Could you call Edith and have her meet us at your house?"

"Of course."

"Give me until noon," I said. "I'm beat."

"We usually go to church at nine, so that will work."

"Fine. I'll explain everything then."

I hung up and had breakfast, then slept for a few hours. When I got up, Clara and Sam had just returned from church. I showered, and while I had a cup of coffee, I told Clara I had to leave again.

"But Dewey, it's Sunday," she said.

"I won't be long." I kissed her. "I'll make it up to you, I promise."

The frown was still on her face when I left.

———

"Ruby told me that the fellow who owns Denver Stamp and Coin was behind all this," Edith said.

"That's right," I said.

I was sitting in the overstuffed chair in Ruby's living room. Edith was sitting on the couch, wearing a fancy black dress with lace and a matching pillbox hat. She nervously fiddled with her gloves.

"Here's coffee for everyone," Ruby said as she came in from the kitchen carrying a tray with three cups and saucers on it. She was also dressed in her Sunday best. She handed me a cup. "It looks like you could use that."

I nodded. "It was a long night."

Edith put her gloves in her lap and took a cup, but she didn't drink it. Ruby sat down, smoothed the front of her dress, and then picked up the last cup. She blew on the steaming coffee for a second, then took a tentative sip.

Edith seemed to be waiting for everyone to be settled, and

then she said, "Okay, quit keeping us in suspense. What happened last night?"

My coffee was hot, so I rested the cup and saucer on my knee.

"Cecil Tipton needed money," I began and told them the whole story as I'd pieced together and as Cecil had confirmed.

"That rat Lester," Ruby said when I finished.

Edith's expression was a mixture of disgust and awe. "I didn't think Lester had it in him."

"I'm not sure he would've actually carried it out without Cecil's help," I said. I took a sip of coffee, then said, "If I had to guess, Lester was wishing he had the guts to blackmail you two, but he didn't do anything until Cecil prodded him forward. When I talked to Lester the other night, he was in a panic."

"He wasn't good at anything," Ruby said, not worried about further tarnishing Lester's already tattered memory.

I changed the subject. "Did your father ever mention hiding coins somewhere around the farm?"

Ruby laughed. "He used to say that he told people that, so they wouldn't think it'd be easy to steal the coins. But no, I have all the coins he had."

I nodded. So Boyd Schuler had wasted his time poking around the Hoffman farm.

"I feel bad," Edith said. "If it wasn't for me..."

Ruby sniffed. "Don't you say that. Lester was his own man, and he made a lot of poor choices, including trying to hurt you."

"If I'd told Gordon, none of this would've happened," Edith said.

I didn't say anything to that. I looked out the window at the street and let the silence sit amongst us, and then I finally turned back to them. "There's one more thing."

"What's that?" Ruby asked.

"Gordon hired me to find out why Edith was acting strangely," I said. "I meet with him tomorrow to update him."

"What are you going to tell him?" Edith asked.

I shrugged at her noncommittally. "What do you think I should tell him?"

She couldn't look me in the eye. "I don't know."

Ruby reached over and grabbed Edith's hand. "Don't you think you should tell him? After all, he's concerned about your well-being. Edith, he loves you."

Edith burst into tears. "What do I do if he decides to leave me?"

"We'll cross that bridge if we come to it," Ruby said. "I've always helped you, and I'm not going to stop now." She sighed, resigned that this was her cross to bear. "Besides, I don't think that will happen. Gordon loves you," she repeated.

I waited uncomfortably until Edith got herself under control.

She sniffled. "I'll think about it."

"But how will Dewey know if you've told Gordon or not?" Ruby asked.

"I'll know by what he says to me," I said.

Ruby arched an eyebrow. "And if she decides not to tell him?"

I smiled. "I'll cross that bridge when I come to it." I stood up to go.

"I can't thank you enough," Edith said.

"I hope things work out for you, whatever you decide." With that, I left.

I was sitting at my desk, jotting down some notes in my journal, when Gordon Sandalwood rushed into the waiting room at half past twelve. As usual, he was impeccably dressed in matching blue. He saw me, and I waved him into my office.

"Have a seat," I said, indicating the chair across from me.

"It's a cold one out there today," he said as he shrugged out of his overcoat. "And lunch-hour traffic was bad."

Although he appeared frazzled from what I suspected was a hurried trip across town, his face appeared calmer than what I'd seen before. He took off his hat, smoothed his hair with one hand, and sat down, holding the coat and hat on his lap.

"So," he announced, "you went from working for me to working for my wife."

I played it cool, but I was secretly pleased that Edith had opened up to Gordon. "What did she tell you?"

"That someone was blackmailing her."

He played with the brim of his hat as he talked, and the whole story came out. Edith had told him everything, including a few details about the affair I hadn't heard from her, and that I wasn't comfortable hearing from him. Some things were better left unsaid. When he finished, he stared down at his hands.

"I'm glad she told me," he said, "but I feel badly that she was scared to. I hope she understands now how much I love her."

"I'm sure she does." And I meant it.

He looked up at me. "We need to settle our account."

I picked up a piece of paper and slid it across the desk. I'd prepared a bill earlier that morning. "My fee and expenses, minus the retainer you already paid."

He stood up, took some cash from his wallet and paid me. He hesitated, as if he wanted to say more, then cleared his throat and said, "Thank you." With that, he abruptly turned and left.

I waited until the outer door closed, then lit a cigarette. The sun came out and a beam of light hit the edge of the desk. I smoked the cigarette while I thought about the case. It had seemed simple, but it hadn't turned out that way. I didn't know what charges Cecil Tipton, Boyd Schuler, and Sonny O'Hara would face, and I was sure I'd end up in court testifying against them. I stared at the money Sandalwood had paid me. I'd be earning it a long time from now.

———

"You actually took a Saturday off," Clara said to me.

I grinned at her. "I told you I would."

It was the following Saturday night, and Clara and I were at the Rainbow Ballroom on Fifth Avenue, where a big band was playing. We were seated at a table near the dance floor, enjoying champagne.

"You've been working so hard lately," she said. Then she laughed. "I know, I should stop worrying."

I winked. "I can take care of myself."

"I know, I can't help myself."

I stood up and held out my hand. "May I have this dance?"

She smiled. "I'd love to."

I led her out to the dance floor, and as we danced, I gazed into her eyes. They didn't carry the sadness they once did, and I wished that someday she could say the same about mine.

"What's wrong?" she asked.

"Nothing," I said.

I smiled back at her, and we danced long into the night. For the briefest time, there were no clients or bills or memories. It was just the two of us.

THE END

215

———

Turn the page for a sneak peek of book 2 in the Dewey Webb Mysteries, *Murder in Fashion*.

SNEAK PEEK

Murder in Fashion, Dewey Webb Mysteries Book 2

Herbert Washburn had been sent to prison two days ago. His crime, murder. So when Helen Washburn, his wife, walked into my office a few minutes after one o'clock on a hot August Wednesday, I was more than a little surprised. The trial was over, her husband convicted. What could she possibly want with a private investigator now?

"Mr. Webb?" she called out, her voice high and tentative, with the hint of a Southern drawl.

I hurried out to the waiting room. "Mrs. Washburn," I greeted her. "Call me Dewey."

Red lips turned into a frown. "You know me."

"I know of you," I said. "You – and your husband – have been in the papers a lot lately."

She nodded as she nervously fiddled with her small purse, her weary brown eyes darting to the small couch and then to the desk that held my typewriter and phone. Probably wondering why a secretary wasn't sitting there. The truth was I couldn't afford a secretary, but I kept up appearances because it made my clients seem more comfortable. Then her tired eyes fell on me.

"My husband asked me to come see you," she finally said.

"I see." I gestured for her to follow me back into the inner office.

I pulled out a club chair positioned in front of my desk, waited until she sank heavily into it, then sat down in my chair and contemplated her. She let out a burdened sigh and met my gaze.

"How much do you know about my husband?" she asked as her fingers continued working on the purse.

I shrugged. "Just what I've read in the papers." She gazed at me expectantly, so I recited the pertinent details of what I knew. "Your husband, Herbert, worked at Templeton Fashion. They're a clothing manufacturer; primarily they design high-end men's suits, but they also do custom work. Herbert worked there until mid-October of last year, when he shot his boss, Melvin Templeton, the president and owner of Templeton Fashion. A jury unanimously convicted him of murder, and he's going to be transferred to a federal prison next week."

"Herb didn't kill Mr. Templeton," she said, her voice raised, but still faint.

"So he maintained all through his trial." I raised my hands, palms up. "But the evidence is against him. It was known around the office that Herb didn't like Templeton, and the week before Templeton was killed, several people saw Herb and Templeton arguing –"

"Yes, and they heard him say he was going to kill Mr. Templeton." She shook her head. "It was an idle threat. Herb would never shoot anyone."

"And yet, when Templeton's body was found, a Smith & Wesson .45 with Herb's fingerprints on it was discovered nearby."

She went from fiddling with her purse to smoothing non-existent wrinkles on her fashionable flowered dress. "I – Herb – couldn't explain that."

"He said someone was trying to frame him."

The muscles in her jaw tightened. "That's right. Herb would never kill anyone," she repeated.

I leaned back and rubbed my chin. "As I recall, Herb said that another worker in the office also hated Templeton, and that maybe he murdered the boss and set Herb up."

"James Lattner. He took care of orders and that kind of thing. People had seen him arguing with Melvin, too."

"But the jury didn't believe Lattner had anything to do with the murder."

She sighed loudly. "I don't know why. He didn't have an alibi for the night Mr. Templeton was killed, and he hated Templeton."

"That wasn't why your husband was convicted." I stared at her. "It was because Herb didn't have a good explanation of why *his* prints were on the gun instead of Lattner's."

"Yes, that was a damning piece of evidence."

I couldn't disagree with that.

"Herb told the jury that he'd had a bad day so he went out, bought a bottle of whiskey, and drank for a while in his car," I said, trying to keep the disbelief from my tone. "Then he went back to the office and passed out at his desk. During that time, he claims that someone shot Templeton, sneaked into Herb's office and put his prints on the gun while he was passed out, and then returned the gun to the crime scene."

"That's what he thinks must've happened."

"And you believe him?"

Her back went rigid. "Of course."

"But no one saw Herb at the office that night, tight or sober," I said.

"I know it looks bad."

That fit Herb's story. He didn't know anything.

"And it wasn't Herb's gun?" I asked.

"He's never owned a gun."

"What did Herb do when he woke up?"

"He came straight home."

"So he said." I gazed at her closely. "Do you remember that night?"

"Of course. He came in a little after eleven. He *was* drunk, and sullen. All he said was work was lousy that day, and he was sorry he was late and didn't call. I fixed him some dinner and left him alone. He ate, then stumbled into the bedroom and went to sleep. And he stayed there until the next morning."

"Was that normal behavior for him?"

She glanced past me. A shadow crossed her face and then was gone. "I wouldn't say normal, but Herb can tie one on once in a while. When that happens, I know to let him be, and he'll be okay."

"Does he ever get ... rough with you?"

"No, he's just moody."

"So there wasn't anything particularly unusual about his behavior that night?"

She hesitated. "He might've been a bit more surly than usual."

I couldn't remember if I'd read that she'd testified to that during the trial, but if she had, it would've only hurt Herb's case.

I thought about what else I knew of the trial. "Herb said he went to a liquor store near Templeton Fashion, but no one at the store remembered Herb coming in to buy the whiskey."

She sighed. "Too much time had passed, and too many people come and go from that store."

"Not only was Herb not seen at the liquor store, he *was* seen near the crime scene."

"Melvin was killed at an office building on the corner of Tenth and Decatur Street, sometime between five, when everyone left, and ten o'clock, when his body was discovered. Around nine o'clock, a woman next door said she saw Herb walk to his car, get in and drive away. Herb said she was lying, but no one believed him."

"She was sure it was Herb?"

She shook her head. "She saw someone dressed like Herb had been that day."

"What's the woman's name?"

She sighed. "Roybal, but at the moment I don't remember her first name."

"What kind of car did she see?"

"A Chevy sedan."

I raised an eyebrow. "What color?"

"Dark, with four doors."

I vaguely remembered reading that. "And that's the kind of car Herb drives," I said, already presuming the answer.

"Yes," she said quietly.

"Did anyone hear a gunshot?"

She shook her head.

I studied this woman, with her stylish clothes yet tired demeanor, her southern drawl so full of indignation. She had no doubt that her husband had not committed the crime he was convicted of.

"Well?" she finally said.

I ticked things off on my fingers. "Someone set Herb up, someone was lying, and no one remembers him where he said he was." Then I stared at her. "It doesn't add up, and that's why the jury found him guilty."

She stayed silent with that.

"And yet he still maintains his innocence."

She nodded. "And he wants you to find the person who did it."

"What makes you and Herb think I can find a killer when the police didn't?"

She let out a bitter laugh. "As you said, all the evidence pointed to Herb. Once the police had their suspect, and the gun with Herb's prints on it, they didn't look anywhere else. And since Herb couldn't explain away the evidence..." Her voice trailed off.

"Why me?" I finally said.

She shrugged. "Your friend Chet Inglewood recommended you."

After I was discharged from the army, I worked as an investigator at the law firm of Masters and O'Reilly. Chet had been their chief investigator and my boss. Chet and I were still friends, and when he could, he sent work my way.

"That was nice of him," I said.

"Please," she begged. "Herb is innocent." She dug into her purse and withdrew a wad of cash. "I have the money to pay you."

"Fine," I finally said. "I'll see what I can do."

We spent a few minutes signing paperwork, and she paid an advance, and then I gathered a bit more information.

"What were Herb and Templeton arguing about?"

"Mr. Templeton said Herb was stealing money from the company, but it's not true. Herb wouldn't do that."

"Did Herb have any coworkers who would vouch for him?"

"He was close to a fellow named Archie Benton. He said a lot of nice things about Herb at the trial."

I wrote it down in a notepad I keep in my pocket. "And no evidence proved that Herb did take any money," I said. She nodded. "Who discovered Templeton's body?"

"Jack Delaney," she said. "He worked at Janosik Tailors, one of the businesses near where Templeton was found. He called the police."

"Do you know what detective worked on the case?"

"A fellow named Emilio Russo."

I'd met Russo a time or two when I worked at the law office. He was tough and didn't take any guff from anyone.

"Besides the gun, what other evidence was found at the crime scene?"

"Nothing," she said. "You can talk to Herb's lawyer. His name is Gil Cassidy."

She gave me his address and phone number, and I jotted that down. I stared at my handwriting for a moment. I didn't have a lot to go on. "Do you work?"

"Not any more. I was a secretary at a doctor's office, until I had Peggy. She's our daughter. She's two. She's been staying with my parents in Texas. We sent her there during the trial because I wanted to be in court with Herb. You can call me at home, anytime you need anything." She gave me the number.

"Is your husband at the Denver County Jail?"

She nodded. "He'll be transferred to prison sometime next week."

I stood up. "I'll do some poking around and see what I can find. I'll call you in a day or two with an update."

For the first time she smiled. "Thank you."

She got up, and I escorted her out to the hallway. Her eyes held relief as she thanked me again. I waited until she went downstairs, and then I went back into my inner office. I spent a few minutes creating a file for Herb Washburn. Then I took a pack of Lucky Strikes from my pocket, lit one, and stared at its glowing end. I used to smoke Camels, but Luckies were included in the C rations I received during the war, and I got hooked on them. Images of the war flashed in my mind, and I forced them back. Then my mind returned to Herb Washburn. I took a drag on the cigarette and thought about him.

There was a very good reason he'd been convicted of killing Melvin Templeton. All the evidence pointed to it. But what if Herb was innocent? Who else had a motive to kill Templeton? I didn't know anything about Templeton, or Herb, for that matter. I was going to have to dig deep for answers. I'd need to talk to Herb, but the first thing I wanted to do was familiarize myself with the crime scene.

I took one last drag on the cigarette, crushed it out, then grabbed my fedora and headed out the door.

———

Click here to download and keep reading
Murder in Fashion, **Dewey Webb mysteries book 2!**

FREE BOOK

Sign up for my newsletter and receive book 1 in the Reed
Ferguson mystery series, *This Doesn't Happen in the Movies*, as a
welcome gift. You'll also receive another bonus!

Click here to get started:
reneepawlish.com/RF2

RENÉE'S BOOKSHELF

Reed Ferguson Mysteries:
This Doesn't Happen In The Movies
Reel Estate Rip-Off
The Maltese Felon
Farewell, My Deuce
Out Of The Past
Torch Scene
The Lady Who Sang High
Sweet Smell Of Sucrets
The Third Fan
Back Story
Night of the Hunted
The Postman Always Brings Dice
Road Blocked
Small Town Focus
Nightmare Sally
The Damned Don't Die
Double Iniquity
The Lady Rambles

A Killing
(Spring 2020)

Reed Ferguson Novellas:
Ace in the Hole
Walk Softly, Danger

Reed Ferguson Short Stories:
Elvis And The Sports Card Cheat
A Gun For Hire
Cool Alibi
The Big Steal
The Wrong Woman

Dewey Webb Historical Mystery Series:
Web of Deceit
Murder In Fashion
Secrets and Lies
Honor Among Thieves
Trouble Finds Her
Mob Rule
Murder At Eight

Dewey Webb Short Stories:
Second Chance
Double Cross

Standalone Psychological Suspense:
What's Yours Is Mine
The Girl in the Window

The Sarah Spillman Mystery Short Stories:
Seven for Suicide

Saturday Night Special
Dance of the Macabre

Supernatural Mystery:
Nephilim Genesis of Evil

Short Stories:
Take Five Collection
Codename Richard: A Ghost Story
The Taste of Blood: A Vampire Story

Nonfiction:
The Sallie House: Exposing the Beast Within

CHILDREN'S BOOKS
Middle-grade Historical Fiction:
This War We're In

The Noah Winter Adventure Series:
The Emerald Quest
Dive into Danger
Terror On Lake Huron

ABOUT THE AUTHOR

Renée Pawlish is the author of The Reed Ferguson mystery series, *Nephilim Genesis of Evil*, The Noah Winter adventure series for young adults, *Take Five*, a short story collection that includes a Reed Ferguson mystery, and The *Sallie House: Exposing the Beast Within*, about a haunted house investigation in Kansas.

Renée loves to travel and has visited numerous countries around the world. She has also spent many summer days at her parents' cabin in the hills outside of Boulder, Colorado, which was the inspiration for the setting of Taylor Crossing in her novel *Nephilim*.

Visit Renée at www.reneepawlish.com.

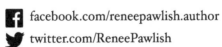

facebook.com/reneepawlish.author

twitter.com/ReneePawlish

instagram.com/reneepawlish_author